RUTABAGA
THE ADVENTURE CHEF

2

Feasts of Fury

ERIC COLOSSAL

AMULET BOOKS
NEW YORK

Cataloging-in-Publication Data has been applied for and may be obtained from the Library of Congress.

Library of Congress Control Number: 2015949580

Hardcover ISBN: 978-1-4197-1658-4
Paperback ISBN: 978-1-4197-1659-1

Text and illustrations copyright © 2016 Eric Colossal
Additional coloring by David McGuire

Printed and bound in China
10 9 8 7 6 5 4 3 2 1

Amulet Books are available at special discounts when purchased in quantity for premiums and promotions as well as fundraising or educational use. Special editions can also be created to specification. For details, contact specialsales@abramsbooks.com or the address below.

ABRAMS
THE ART OF BOOKS SINCE 1949
115 West 18th Street
New York, NY 10011
www.abramsbooks.com

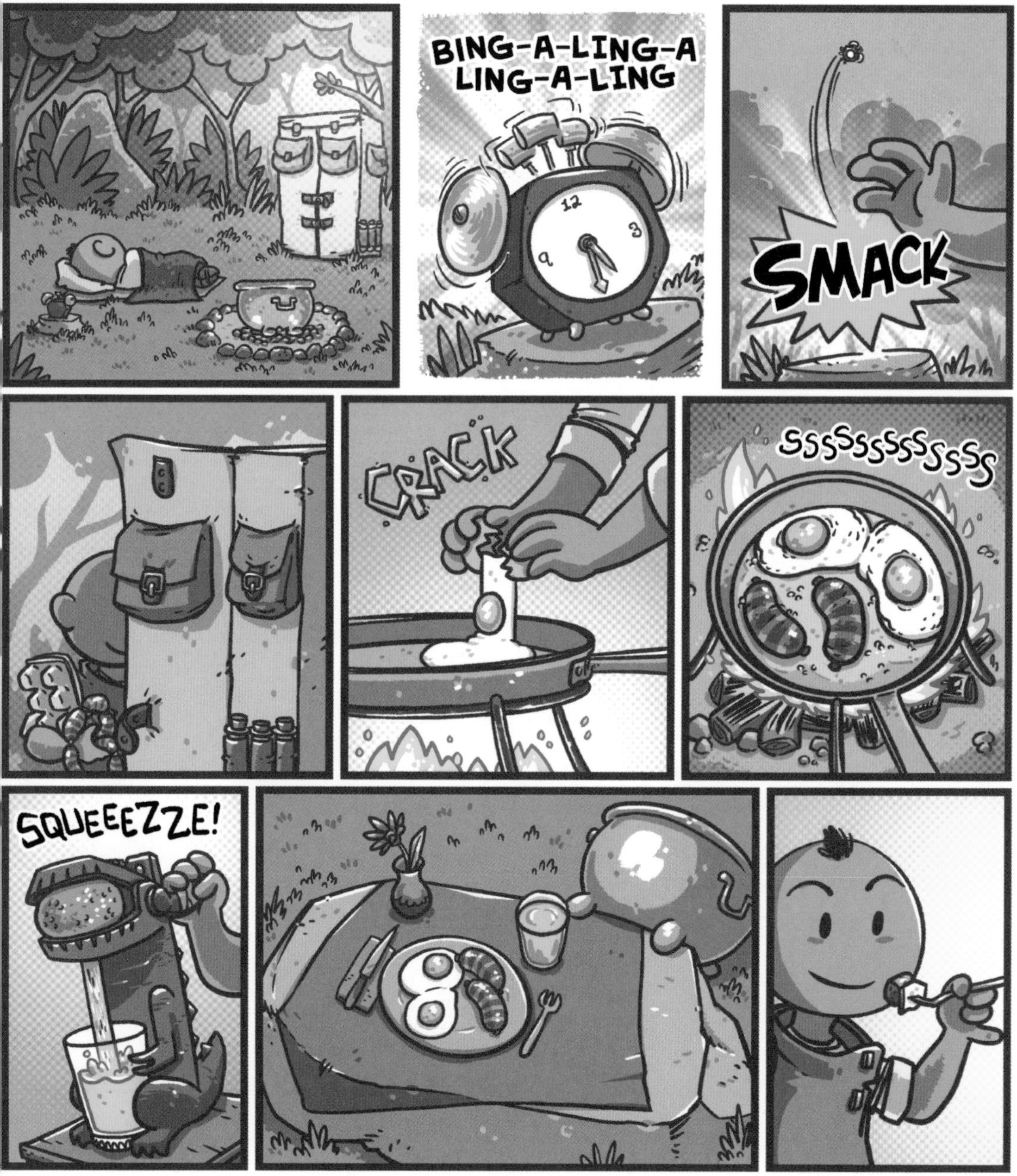
BING-A-LING-A
LING-A-LING
SMACK
CRACK
SSSSSSSSSSSSSS
SQUEEEZZE!

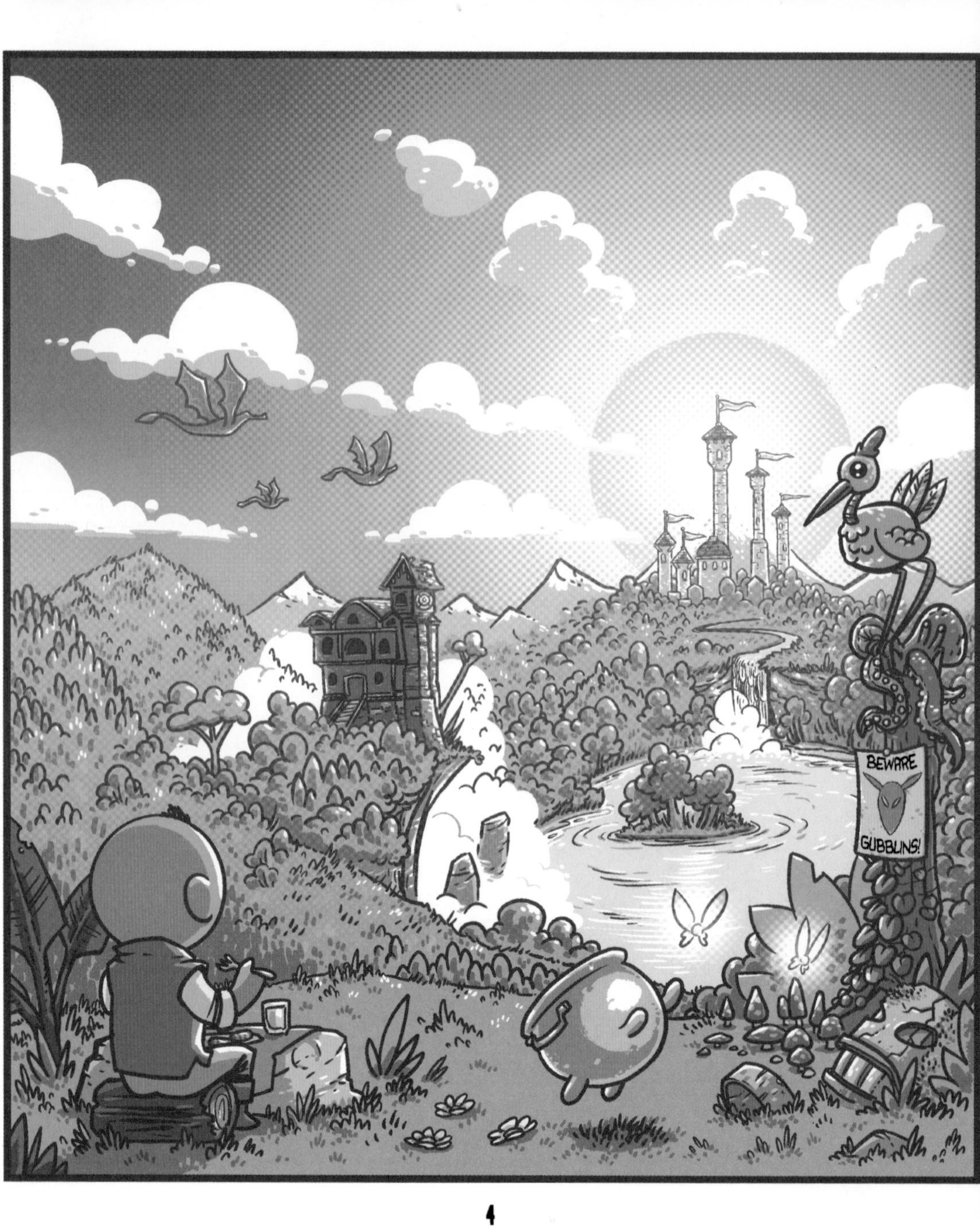
BEWARE
GUBBLINS!

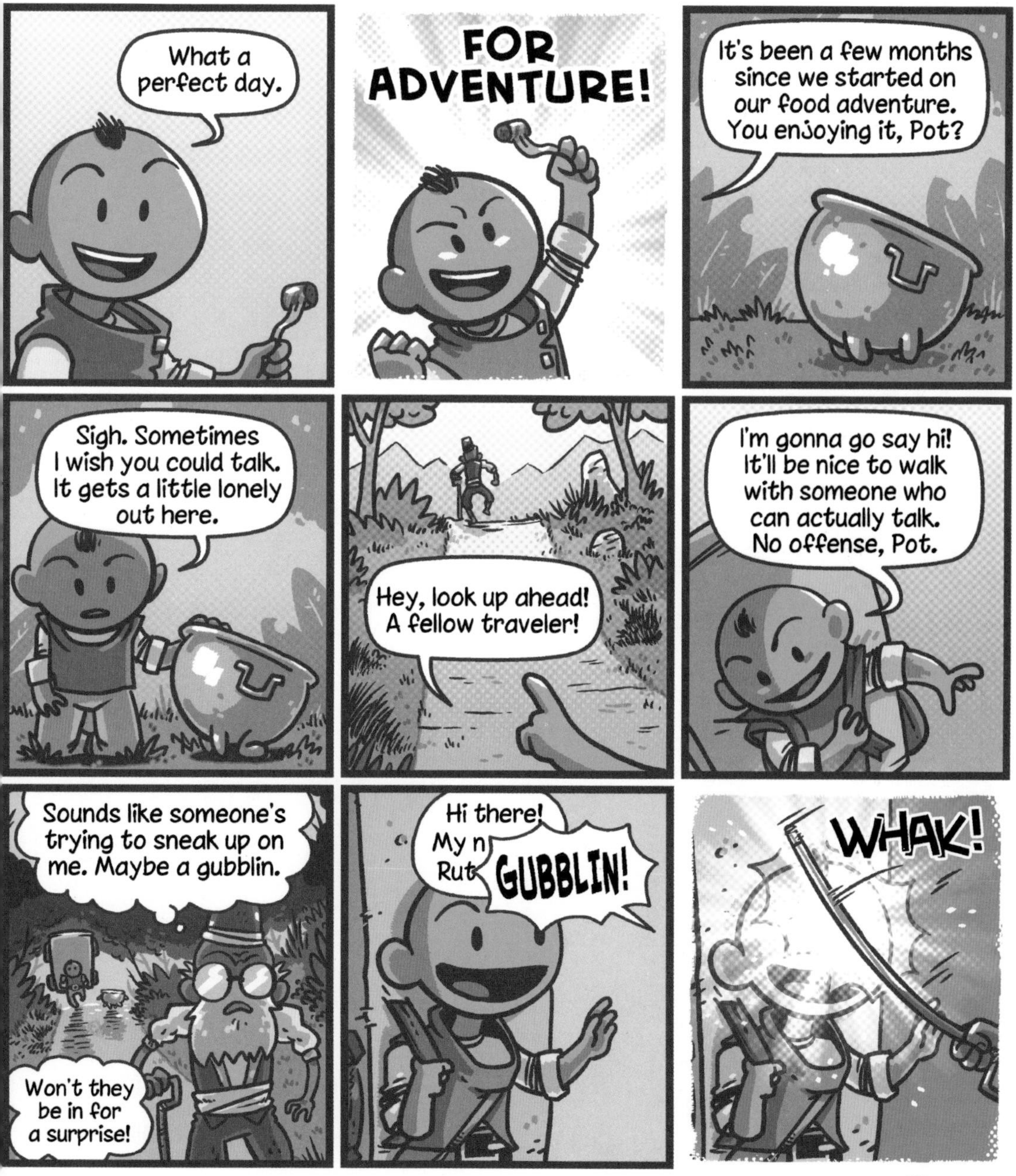
What a perfect day.
FOR ADVENTURE!
It's been a few months since we started on our food adventure. You enjoying it, Pot?
Sigh. Sometimes I wish you could talk. It gets a little lonely out here.
Hey, look up ahead! A fellow traveler!
I'm gonna go say hi! It'll be nice to walk with someone who can actually talk. No offense, Pot.
Sounds like someone's trying to sneak up on me. Maybe a gubblin.
Won't they be in for a surprise!
Hi there! My n
Rut
GUBBLIN!
WHAK!

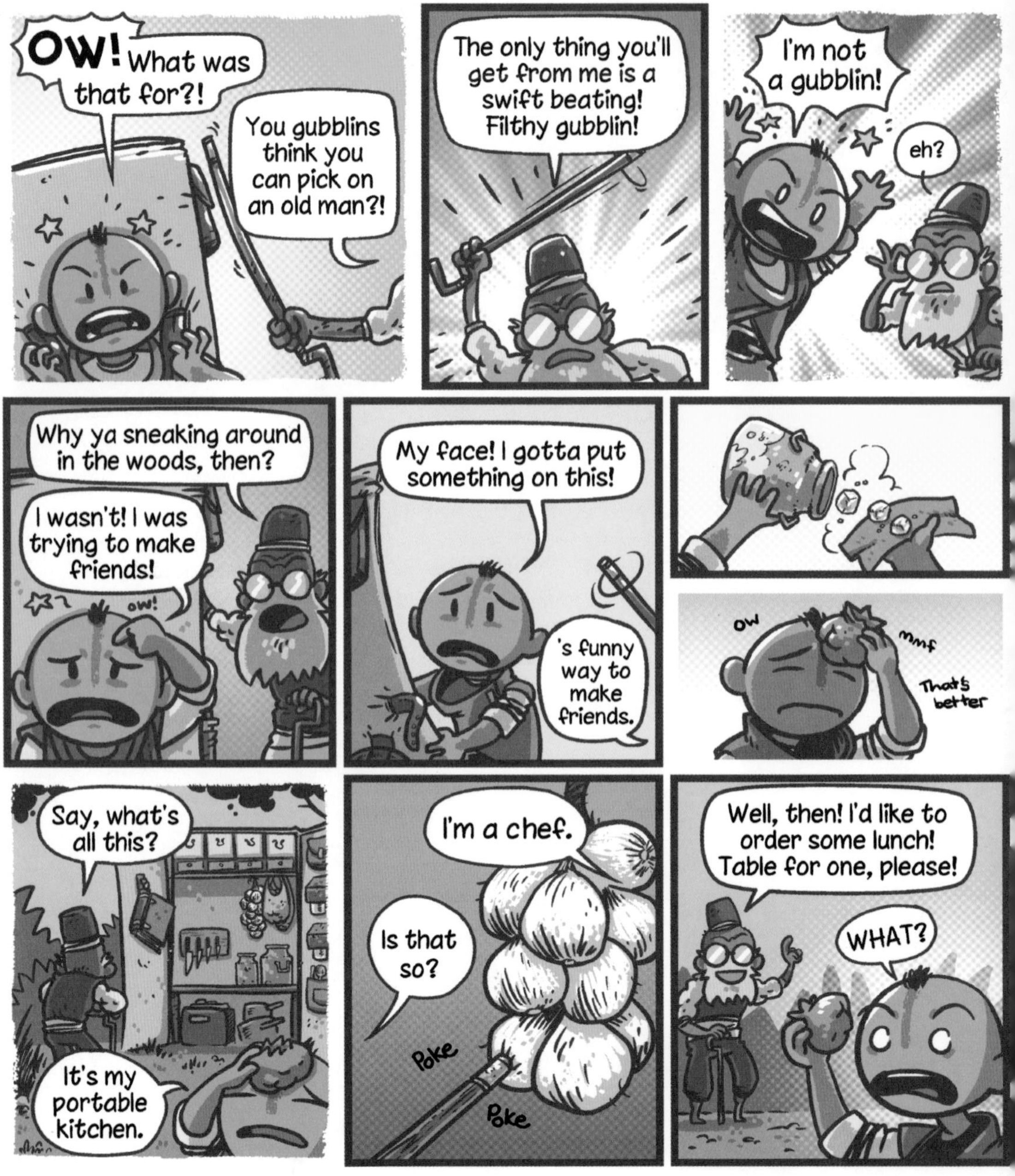
OW! What was that for?!
You gubblins think you can pick on an old man?!
The only thing you'll get from me is a swift beating! Filthy gubblin!
I'm not a gubblin!
eh?
Why ya sneaking around in the woods, then?
I wasn't! I was trying to make friends!
OW!
My face! I gotta put something on this!
's funny way to make friends.
OW
mmf
That's better
Say, what's all this?
It's my portable kitchen.
I'm a chef.
Is that so?
POKE
POKE
Well, then! I'd like to order some lunch! Table for one, please!
WHAT?

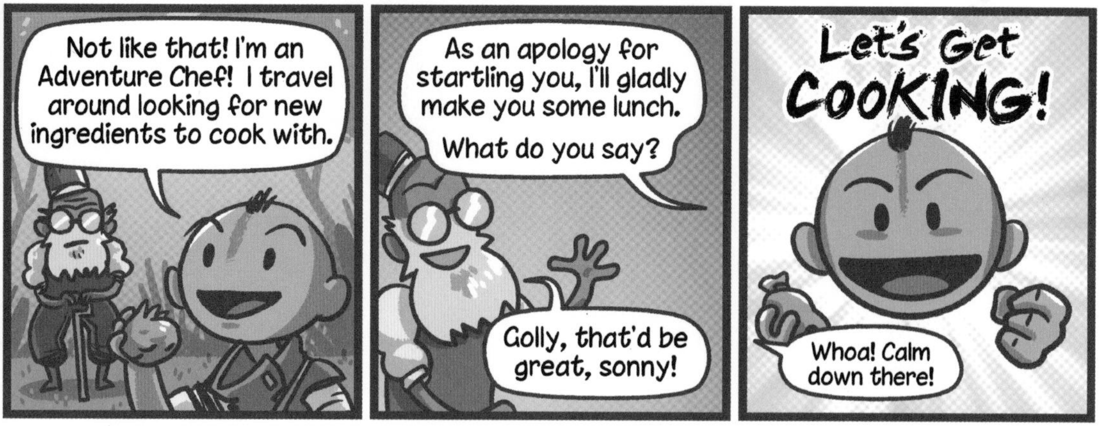
Not like that! I'm an Adventure Chef! I travel around looking for new ingredients to cook with.
As an apology for startling you, I'll gladly make you some lunch.
What do you say?
Golly, that'd be great, sonny!
Let's Get COOKING!
Whoa! Calm down there!

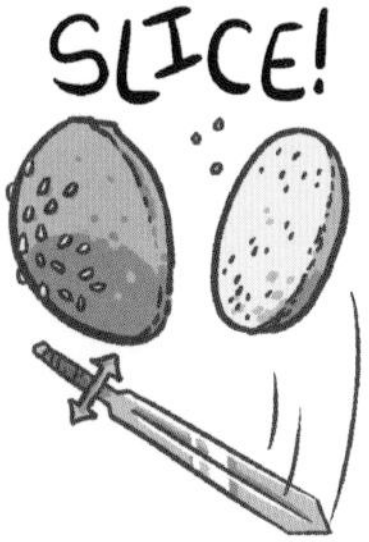
SLICE!

1. Cut a nice crusty roll in half.

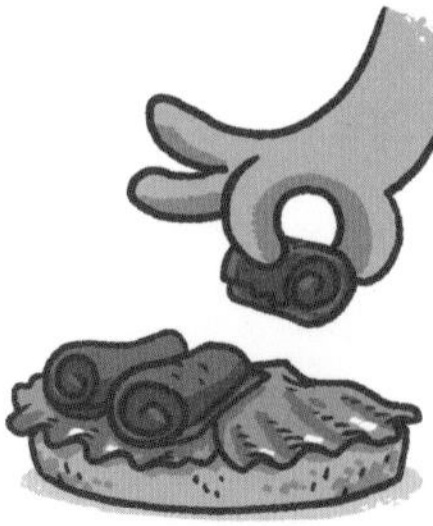

2. Add lettuce and rolls of lunch meat.

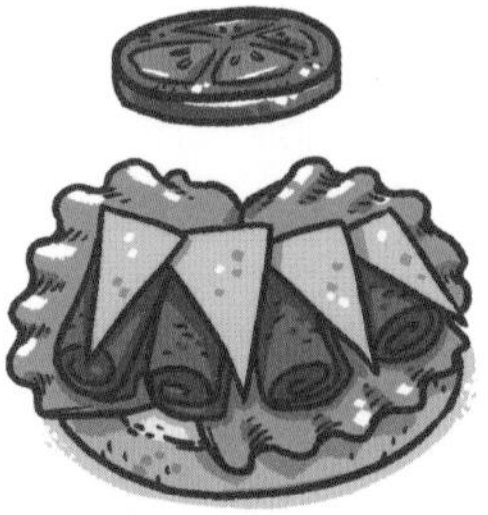

3. Cut cheese into triangles and place on roll. Add a tomato.

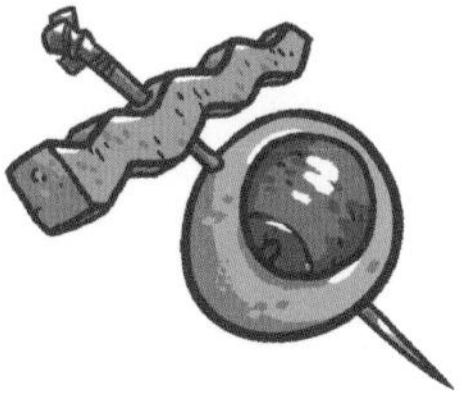

4. Spear 2 olives and crinkle-cut carrots with toothpicks.

You have made a . . .

SANDWICH MONSTER

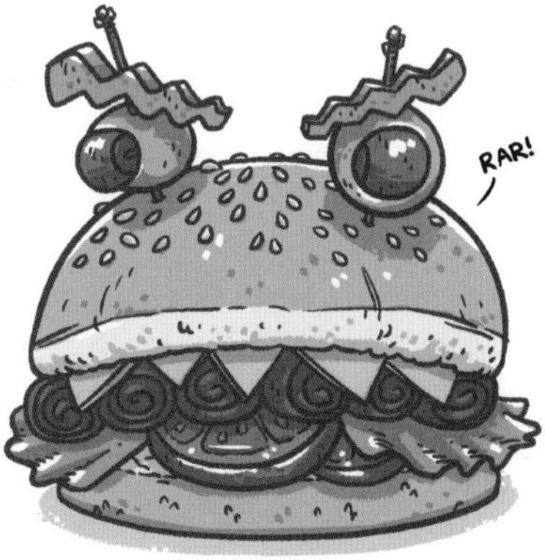
RAR!

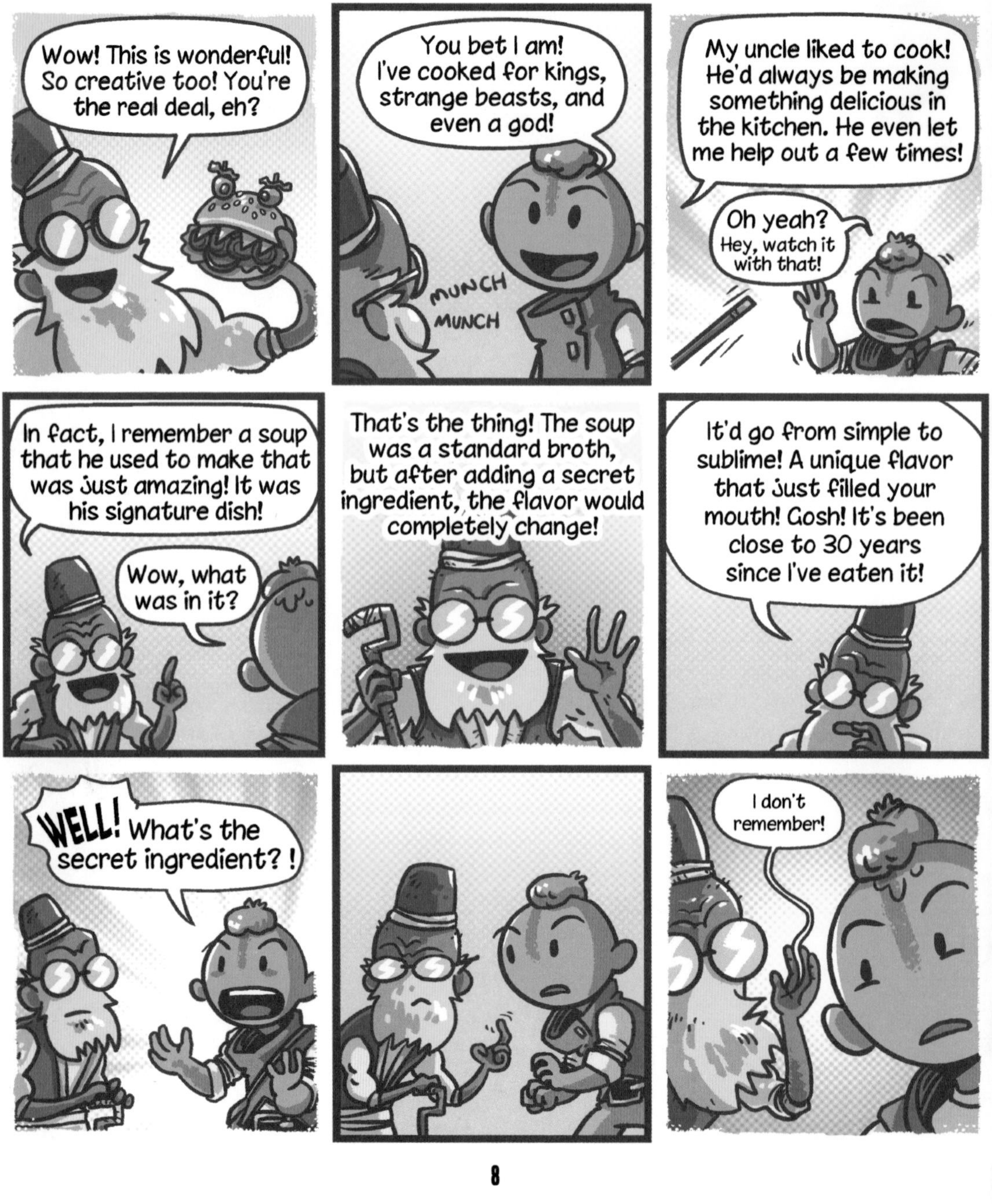
Wow! This is wonderful! So creative too! You're the real deal, eh?
You bet I am! I've cooked for kings, strange beasts, and even a god!
MUNCH MUNCH
My uncle liked to cook! He'd always be making something delicious in the kitchen. He even let me help out a few times!
Oh yeah? Hey, watch it with that!
In fact, I remember a soup that he used to make that was just amazing! It was his signature dish!
Wow, what was in it?
That's the thing! The soup was a standard broth, but after adding a secret ingredient, the flavor would completely change!
It'd go from simple to sublime! A unique flavor that just filled your mouth! Gosh! It's been close to 30 years since I've eaten it!
WELL! What's the secret ingredient?!
I don't remember!

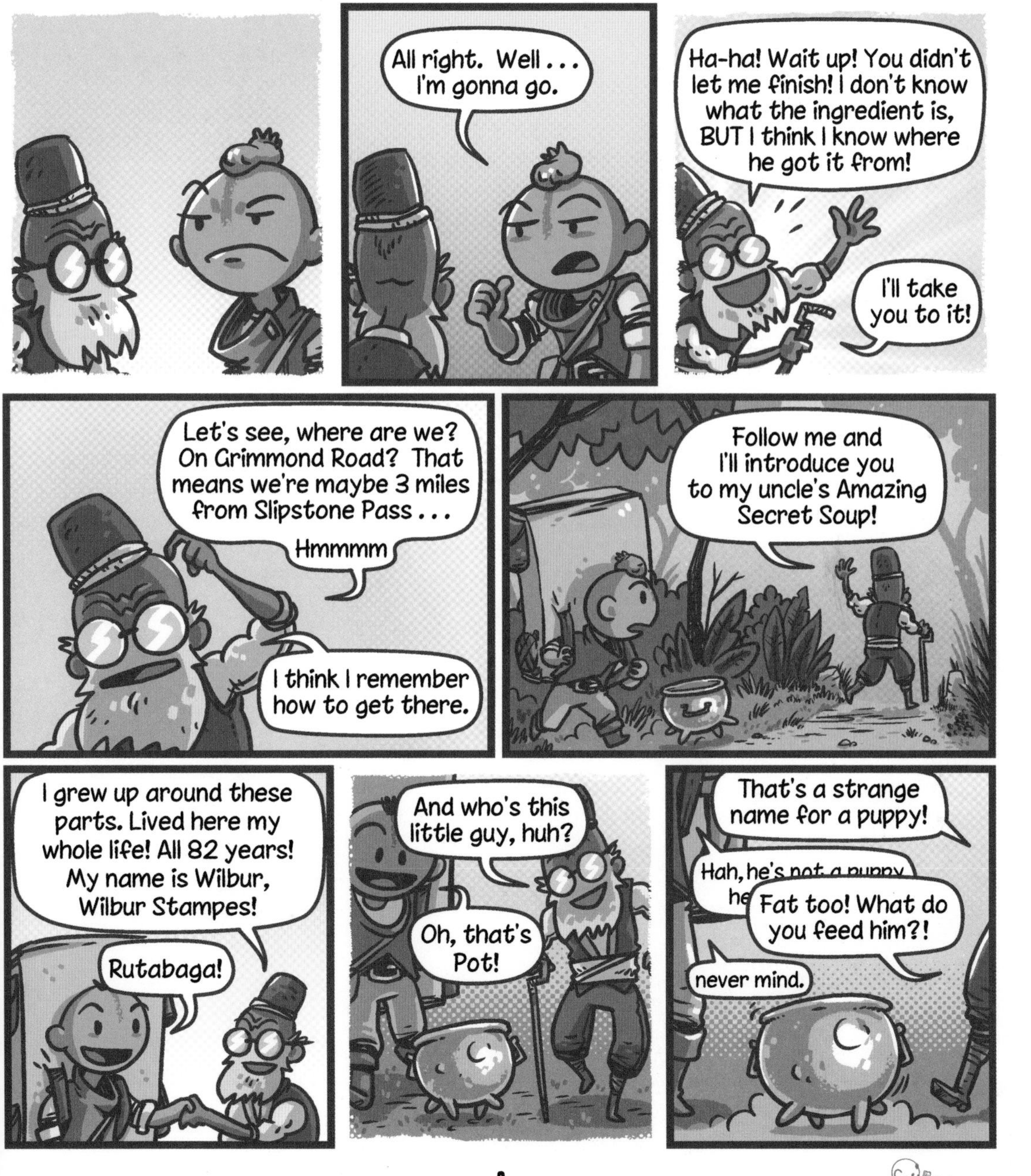
All right. Well . . .
I'm gonna go.
Ha-ha! Wait up! You didn't let me finish! I don't know what the ingredient is, BUT I think I know where he got it from!
I'll take you to it!
Let's see, where are we? On Grimmond Road? That means we're maybe 3 miles from Slipstone Pass . . .
Hmmmm
I think I remember how to get there.
Follow me and I'll introduce you to my uncle's Amazing Secret Soup!
I grew up around these parts. Lived here my whole life! All 82 years! My name is Wilbur, Wilbur Stampes!
Rutabaga!
And who's this little guy, huh?
Oh, that's Pot!
That's a strange name for a puppy!
Fat too! What do you feed him?!
never mind.

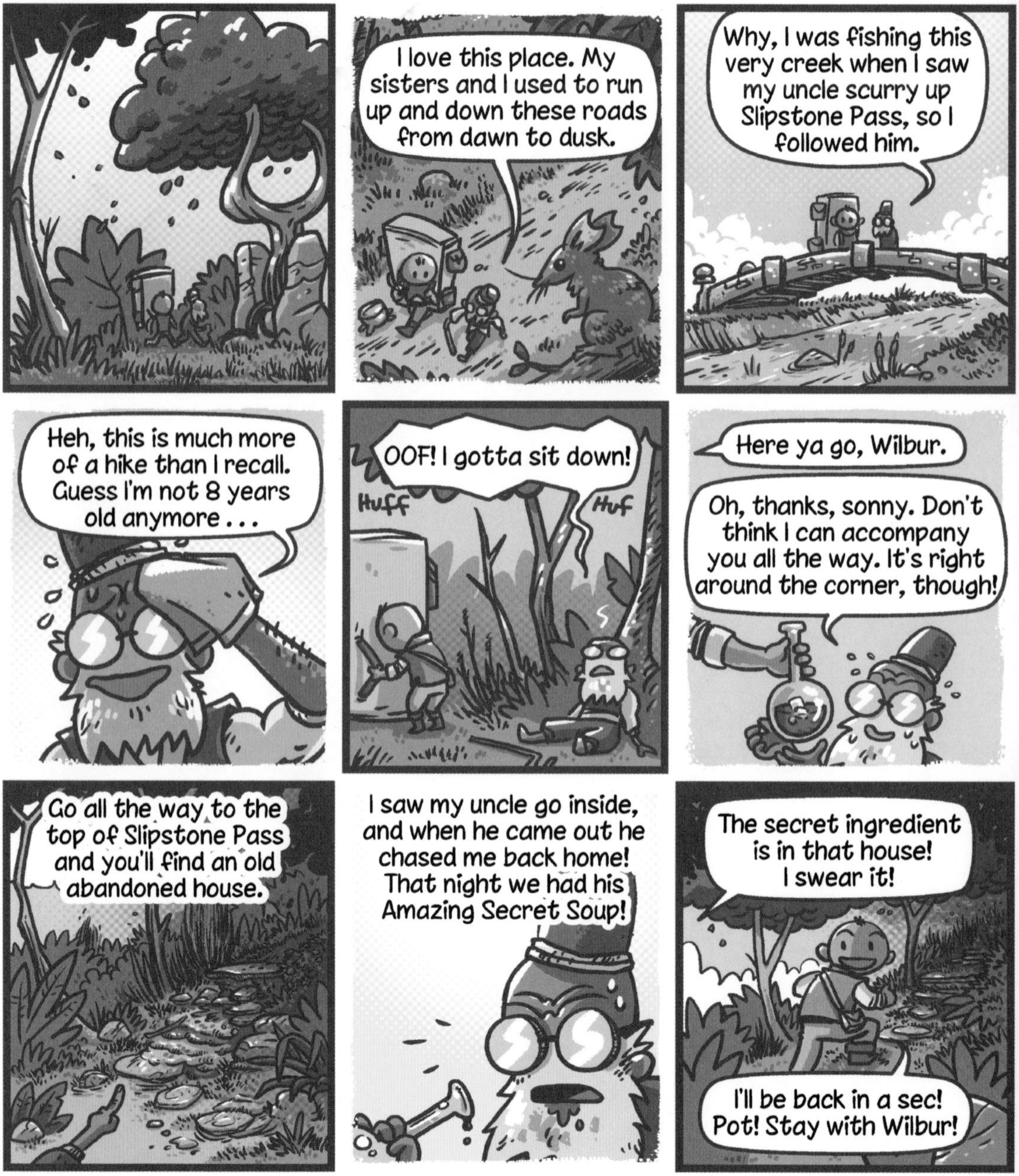
I love this place. My sisters and I used to run up and down these roads from dawn to dusk.
Why, I was fishing this very creek when I saw my uncle scurry up Slipstone Pass, so I followed him.
Heh, this is much more of a hike than I recall. Guess I'm not 8 years old anymore . . .
OOF! I gotta sit down!
Huff
Huf
Here ya go, Wilbur.
Oh, thanks, sonny. Don't think I can accompany you all the way. It's right around the corner, though!
Go all the way to the top of Slipstone Pass and you'll find an old abandoned house.
I saw my uncle go inside, and when he came out he chased me back home! That night we had his Amazing Secret Soup!
The secret ingredient is in that house! I swear it!
I'll be back in a sec! Pot! Stay with Wilbur!

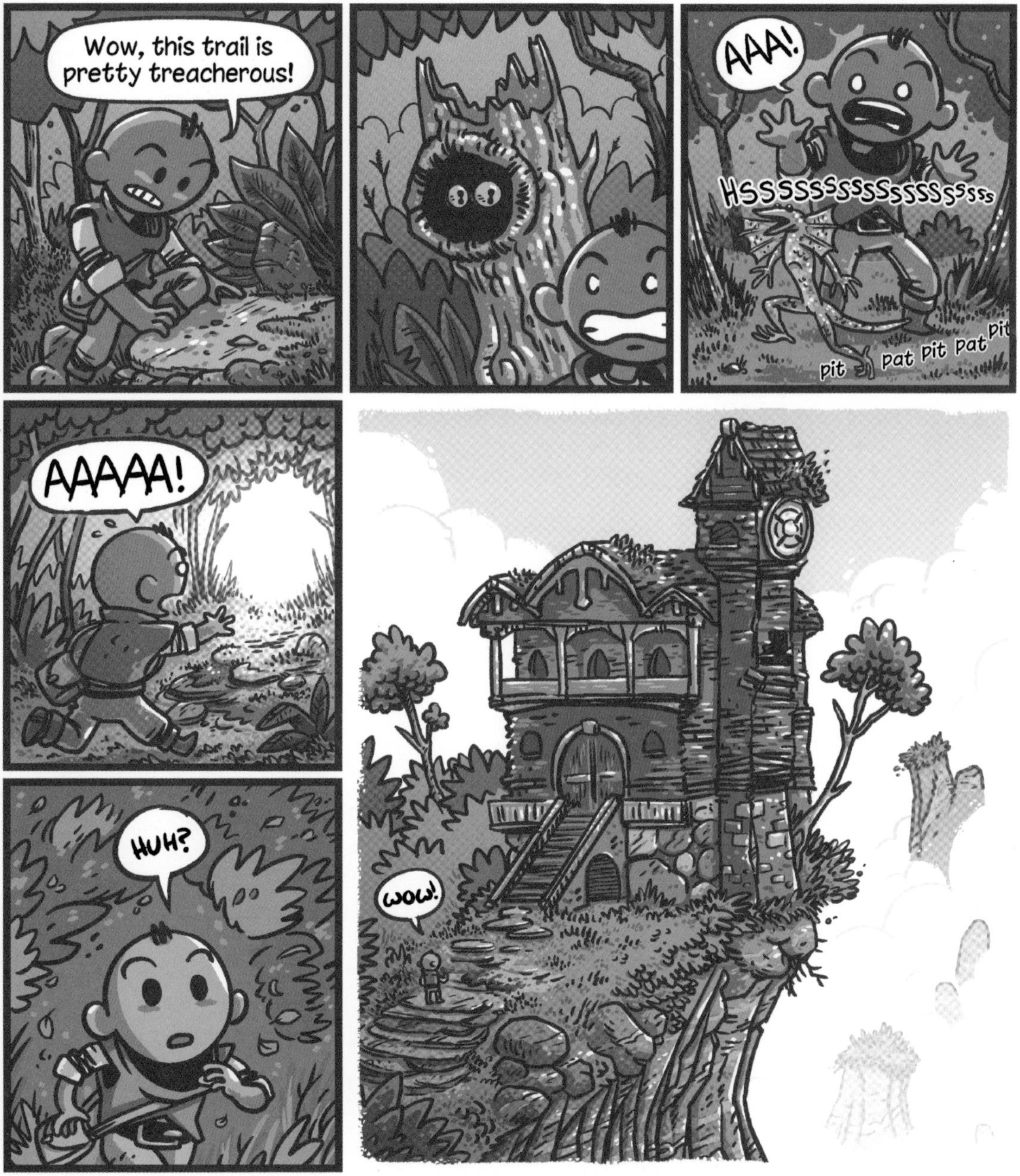
Wow, this trail is pretty treacherous!
AAA!
HSSSSSSSSSSSSSSSSSsss
pit pat pit pat pit
AAAAA!
HUH?
WOW!

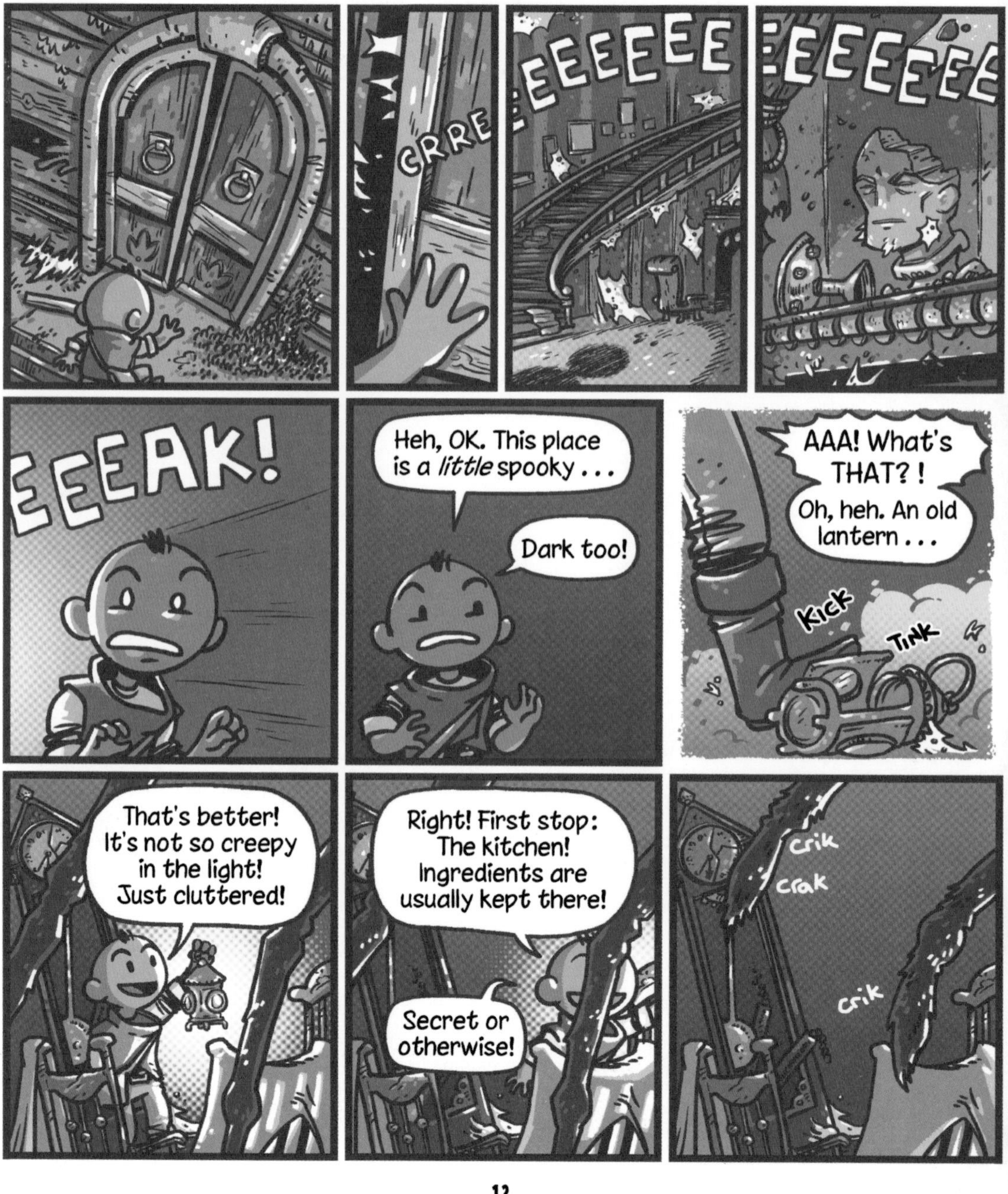
CRREEEEEEEEEEEEEEEEEEEEEEEAK!
Heh, OK. This place is a *little* spooky . . .
Dark too!
AAA! What's THAT? !
Oh, heh. An old lantern . . .
KICK
TINK
That's better! It's not so creepy in the light! Just cluttered!
Right! First stop: The kitchen! Ingredients are usually kept there!
Secret or otherwise!
crik
crak
crik

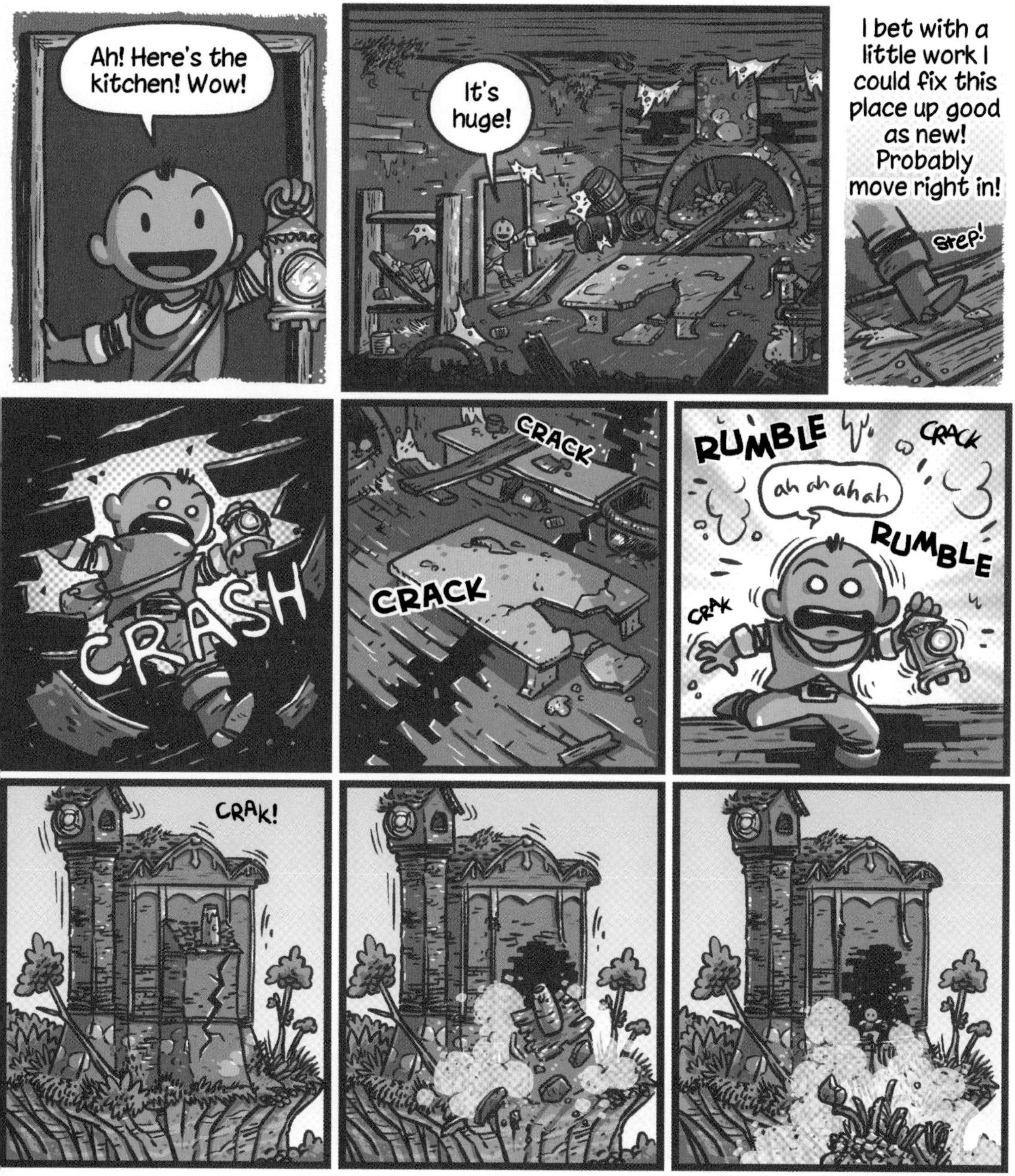

Ah! Here's the kitchen! Wow!
It's huge!
I bet with a little work I could fix this place up good as new! Probably move right in!
STEP!
CRASH
CRACK
CRACK
RUMBLE
CRACK
ah ah ah ah
RUMBLE
CRAK
CRAK!

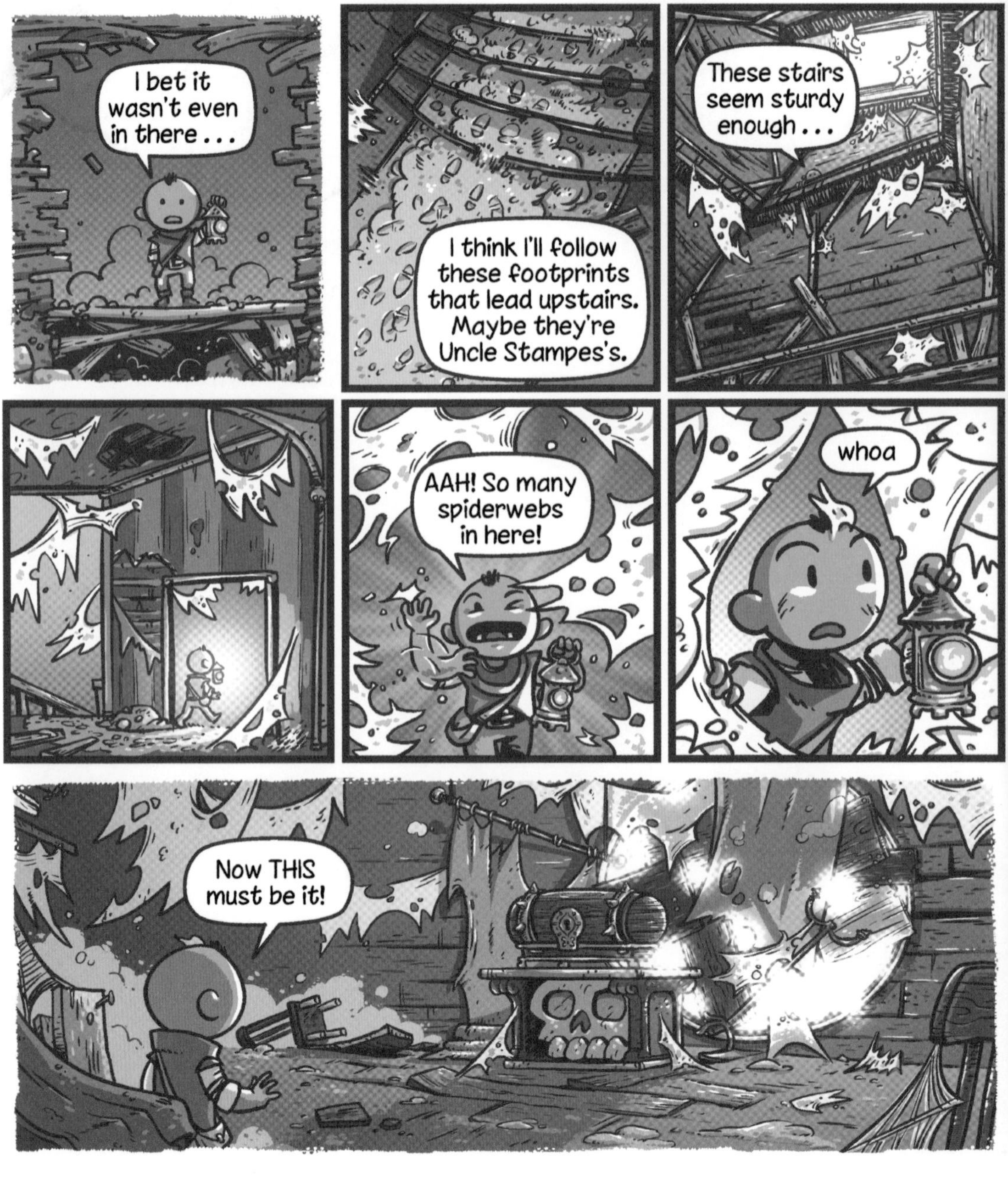
I bet it wasn't even in there . . .
I think I'll follow these footprints that lead upstairs. Maybe they're Uncle Stampes's.
These stairs seem sturdy enough . . .
AAH! So many spiderwebs in here!
whoa
Now THIS must be it!

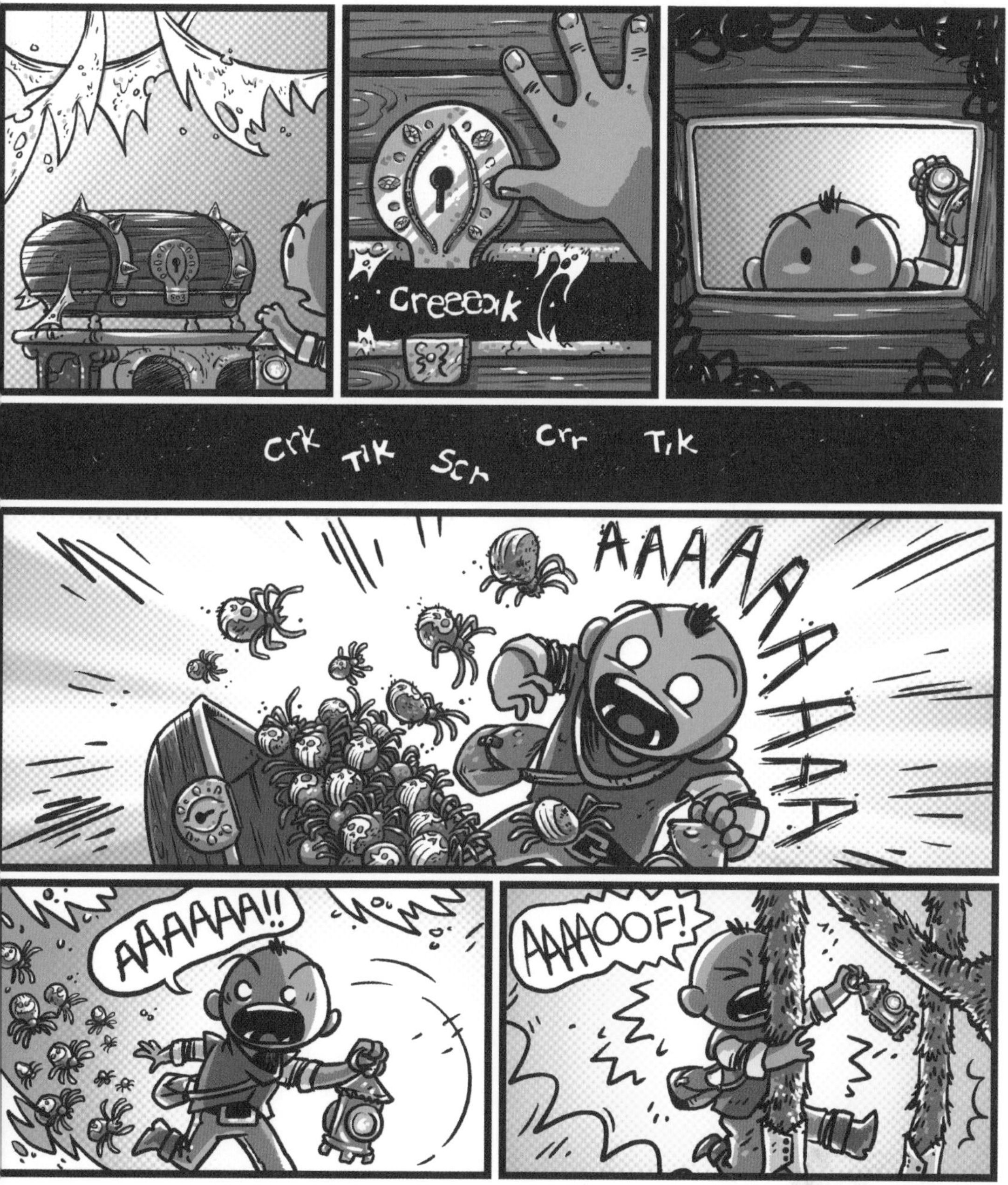
Creeeak
Crk
Tik
Scr
Crr
Tik
AAAAAAAAAAAA
AAAAAA!!
AAAAOOF!

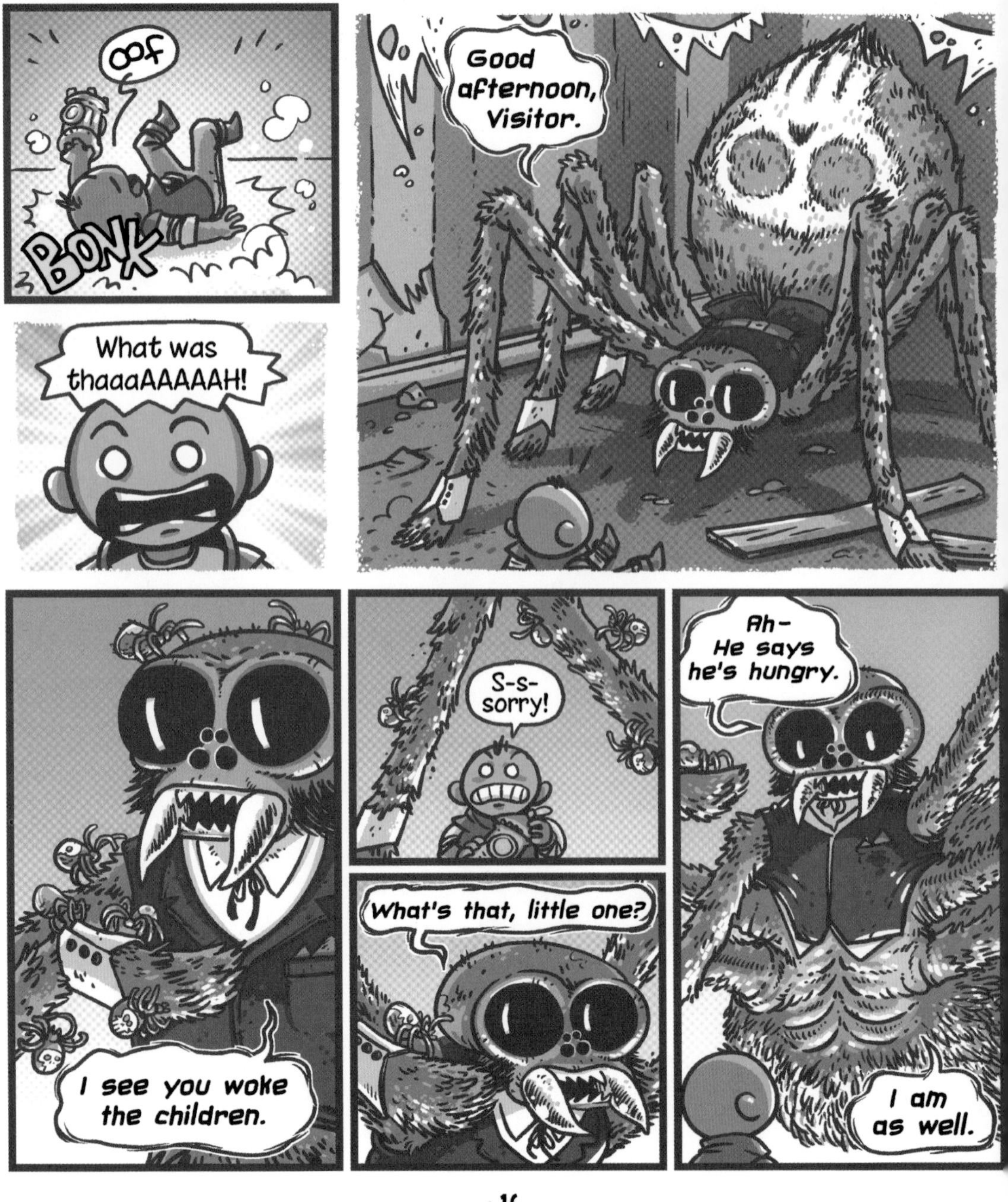
OOF
BONK
What was thaaaAAAAAH!
Good afternoon, Visitor.
I see you woke the children.
S-s-sorry!
What's that, little one?
Ah- He says he's hungry.
I am as well.

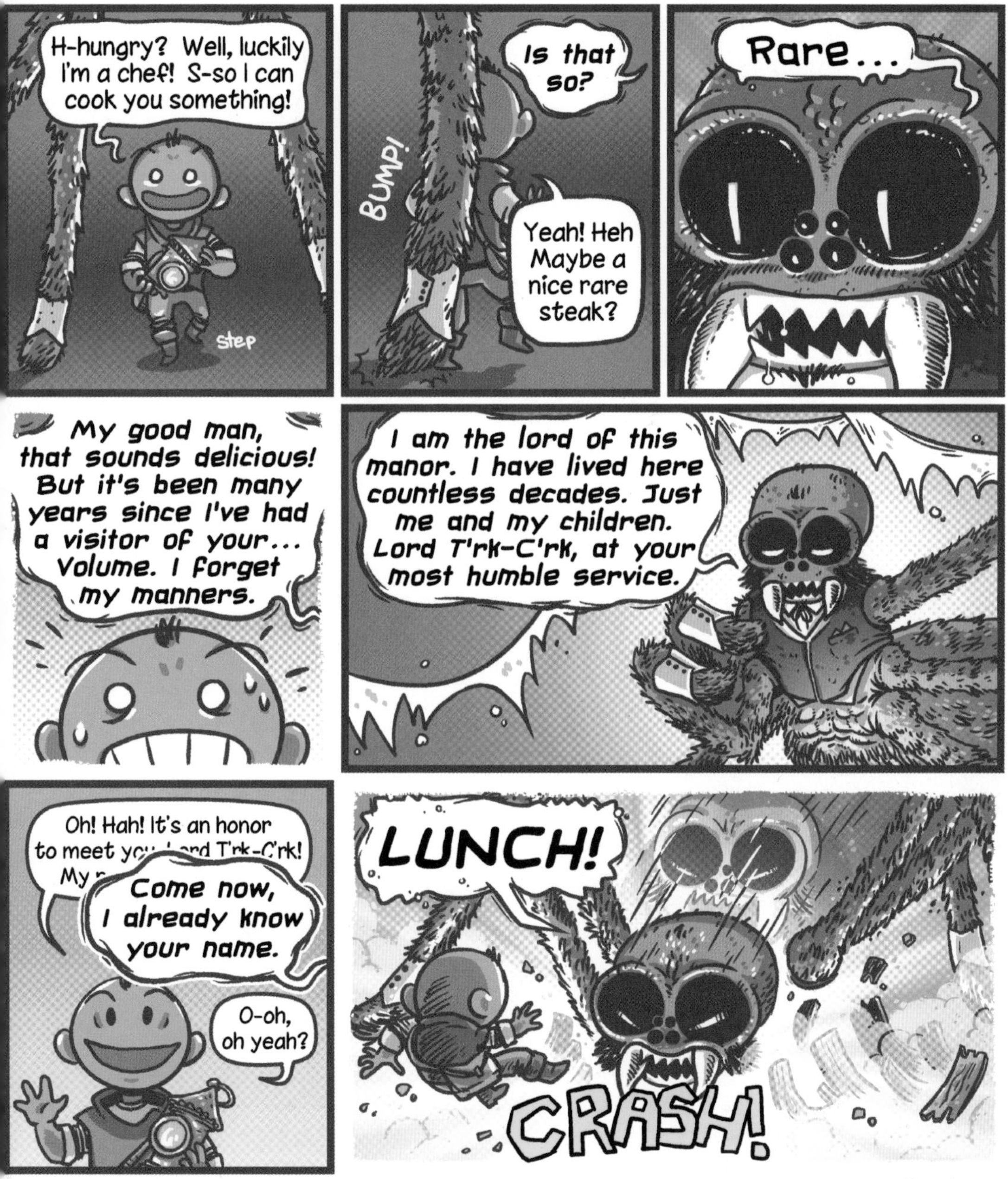
H-hungry? Well, luckily I'm a chef! S-so I can cook you something!
step
Is that so?
BUMP!
Yeah! Heh Maybe a nice rare steak?
Rare...
My good man, that sounds delicious! But it's been many years since I've had a visitor of your... Volume. I forget my manners.
I am the lord of this manor. I have lived here countless decades. Just me and my children. Lord T'rk-C'rk, at your most humble service.
Oh! Hah! It's an honor to meet yo
Come now, I already know your name.
O-oh, oh yeah?
LUNCH!
CRASH!

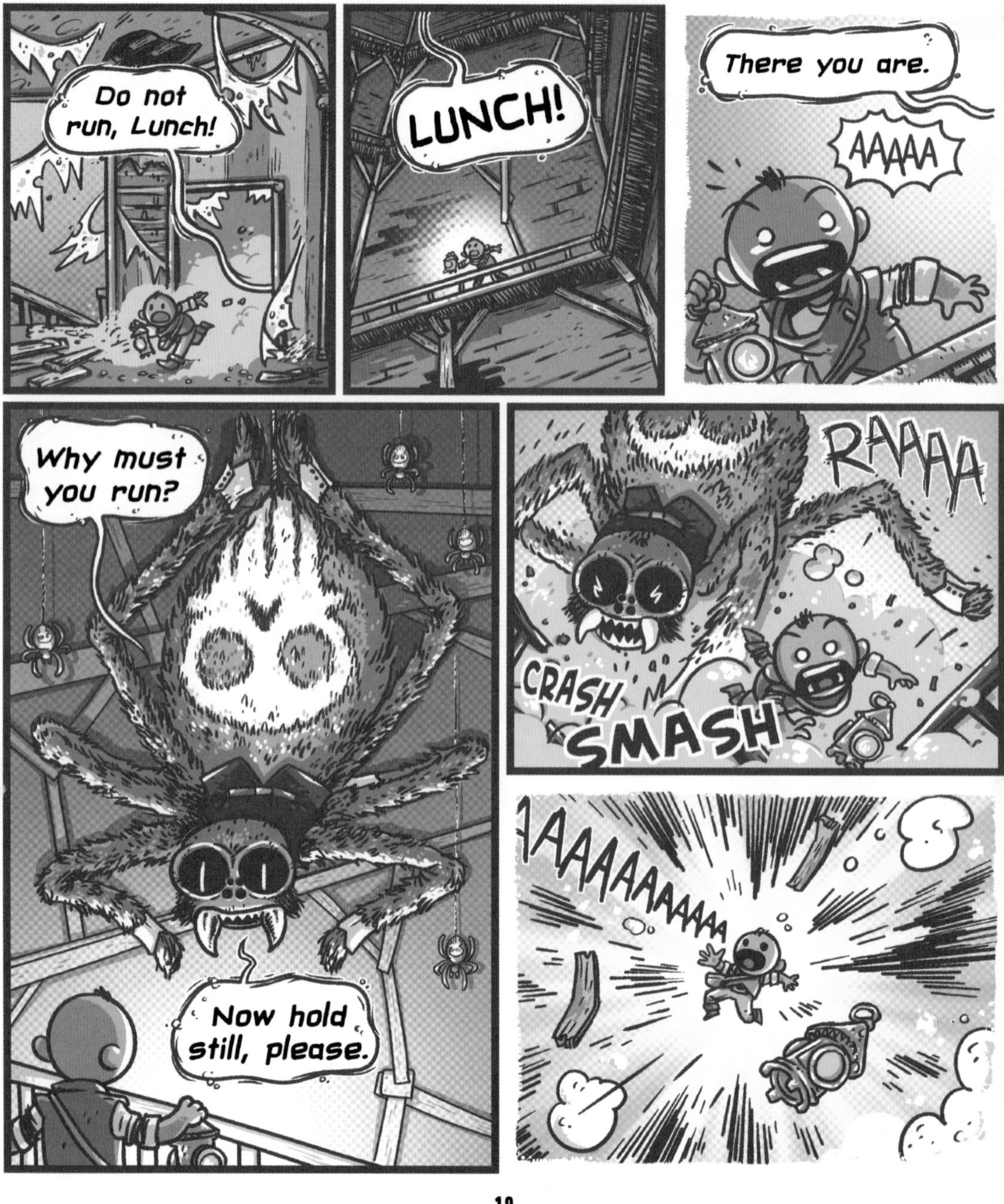
Do not run, Lunch!
LUNCH!
There you are.
AAAAA
Why must you run?
Now hold still, please.
RAAAAA
CRASH
SMASH
AAAAAAAAAAAA

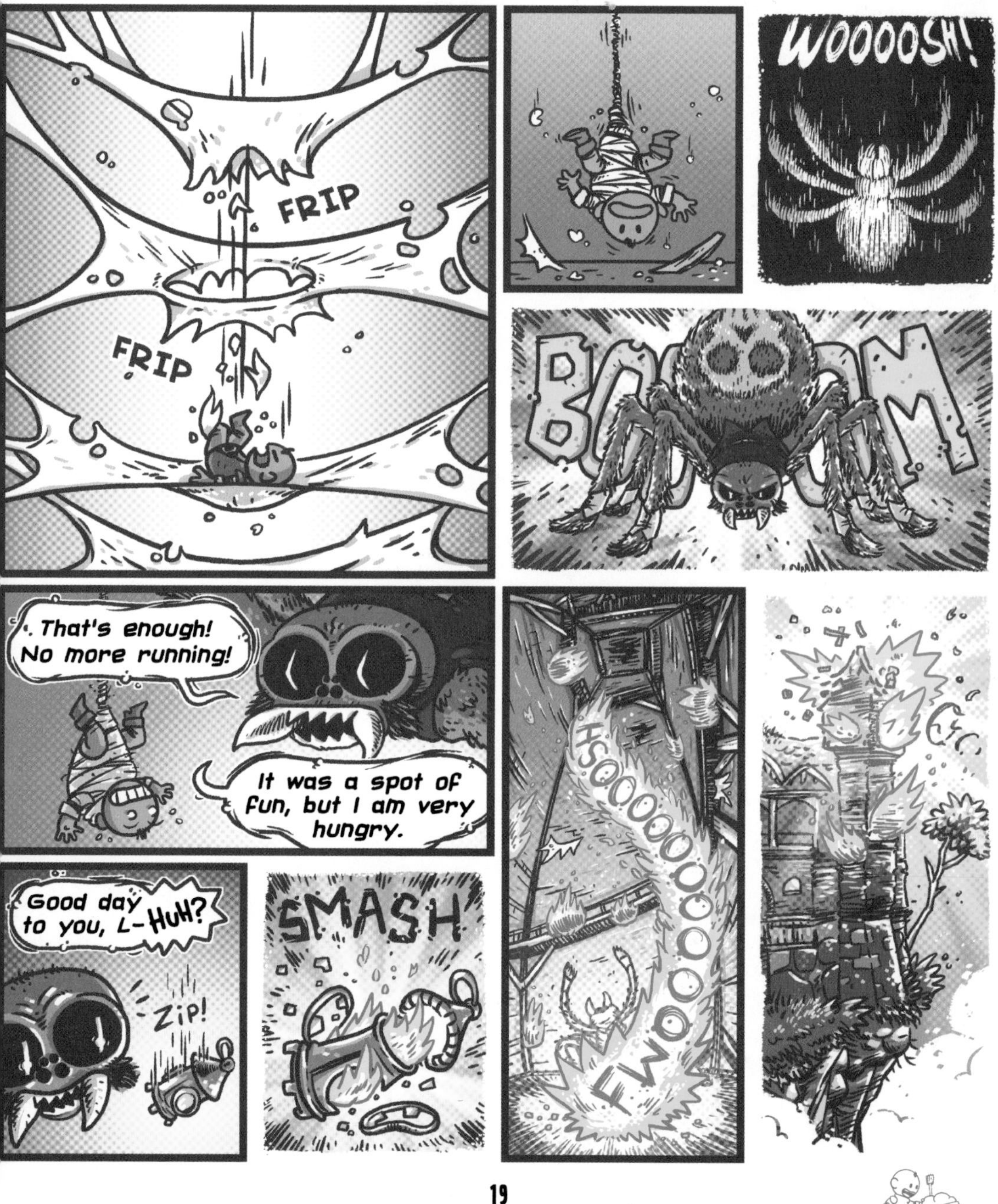
FRIP
FRIP
WOOOOSH!
BOOOOM
That's enough! No more running!
It was a spot of fun, but I am very hungry.
Good day to you, L- HUH?
ZIP!
SMASH
FWOOOOOOOOOOSH

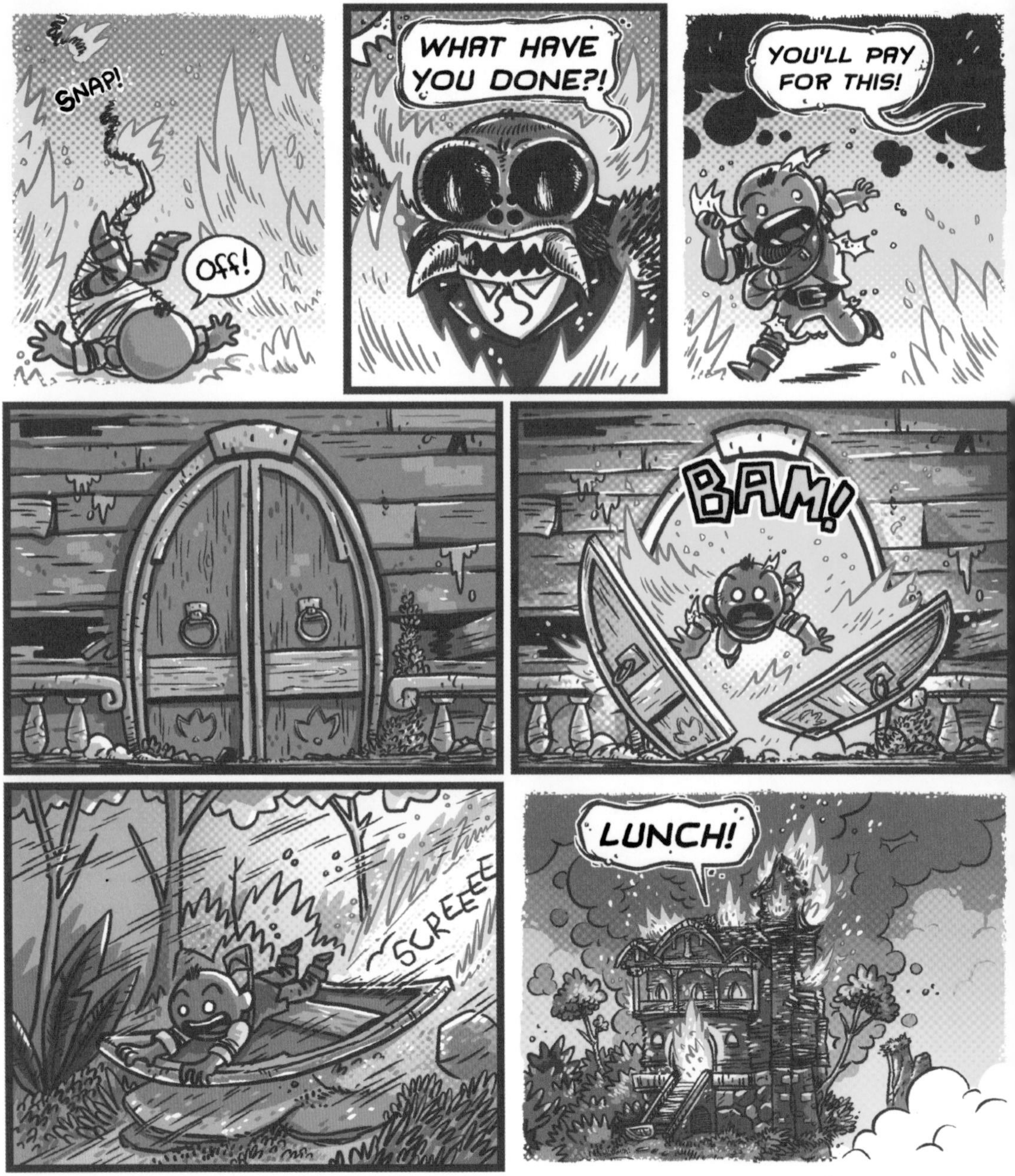
SNAP!
Off!
WHAT HAVE YOU DONE?!
YOU'LL PAY FOR THIS!
BAM!
SCREEEE
LUNCH!

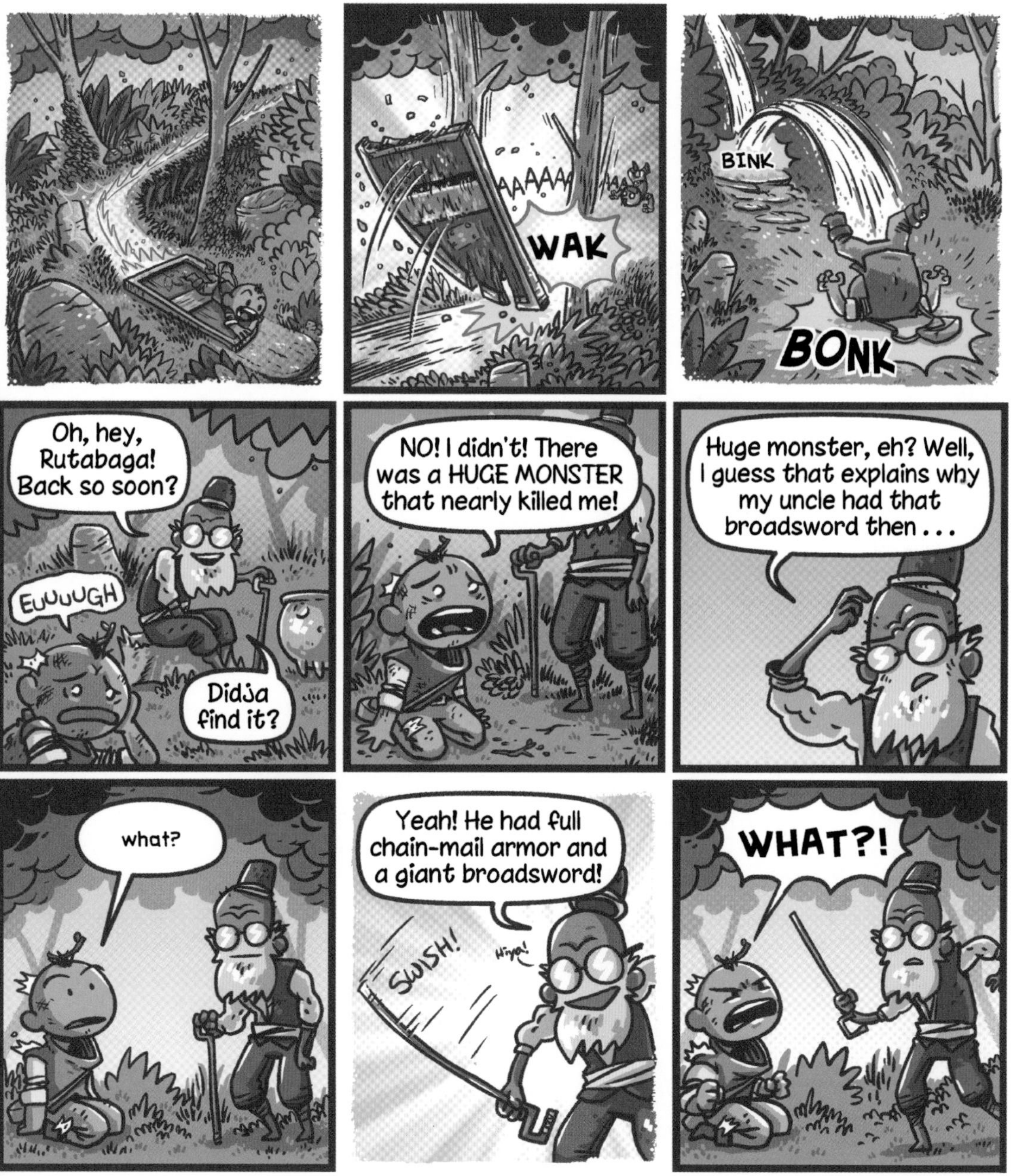
AAAAAA
WAK
BINK
BONK
Oh, hey, Rutabaga! Back so soon?
EUUUUGH
Didja find it?
NO! I didn't! There was a HUGE MONSTER that nearly killed me!
Huge monster, eh? Well, I guess that explains why my uncle had that broadsword then . . .
what?
Yeah! He had full chain-mail armor and a giant broadsword!
SWISH!
Hiya!
WHAT?!

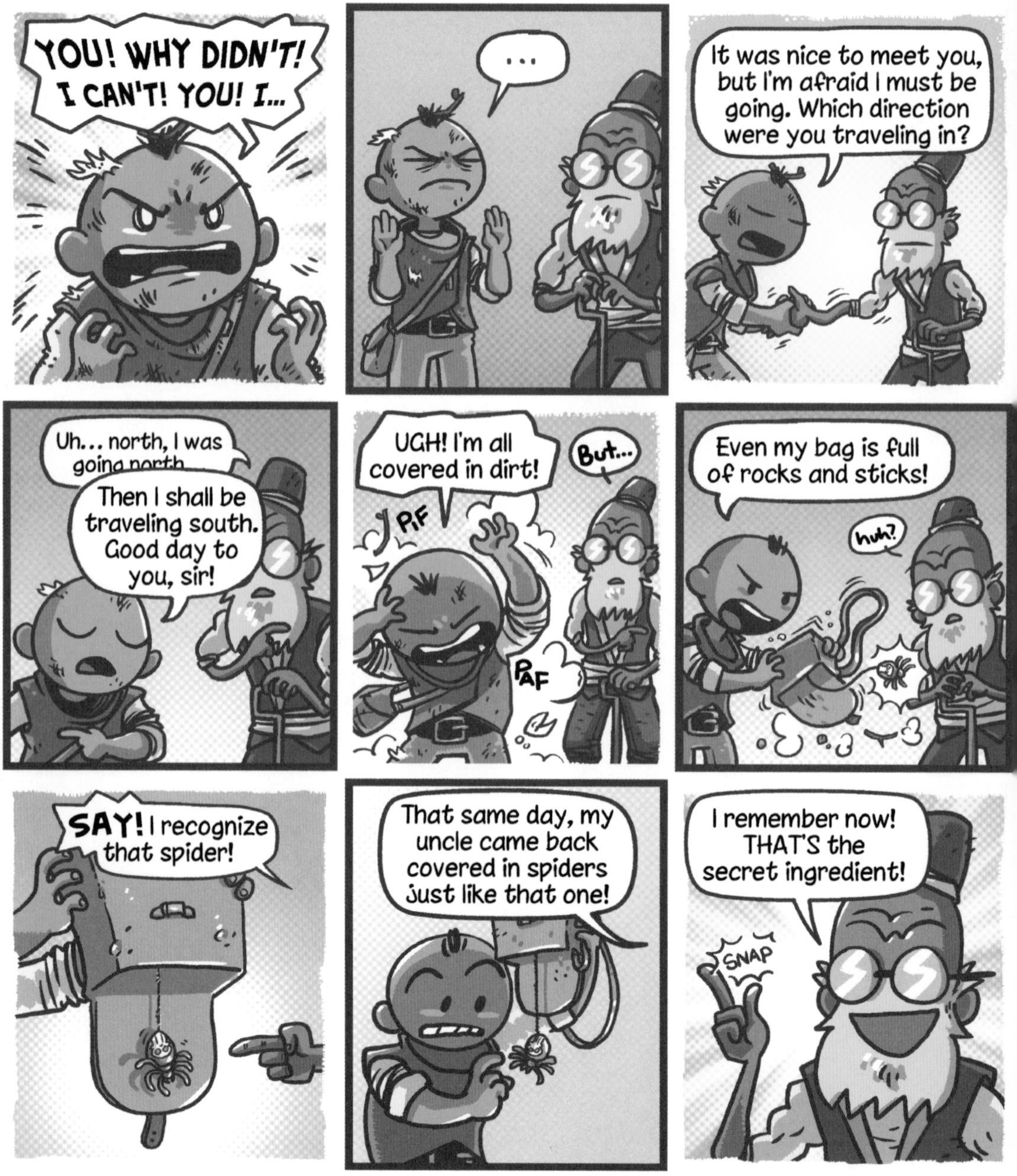

YOU! WHY DIDN'T! I CAN'T! YOU! I...
...
It was nice to meet you, but I'm afraid I must be going. Which direction were you traveling in?
Uh... north, I was going north...
Then I shall be traveling south. Good day to you, sir!
UGH! I'm all covered in dirt!
But...
PIF
PAF
Even my bag is full of rocks and sticks!
huh?
SAY! I recognize that spider!
That same day, my uncle came back covered in spiders just like that one!
I remember now! THAT'S the secret ingredient!
SNAP

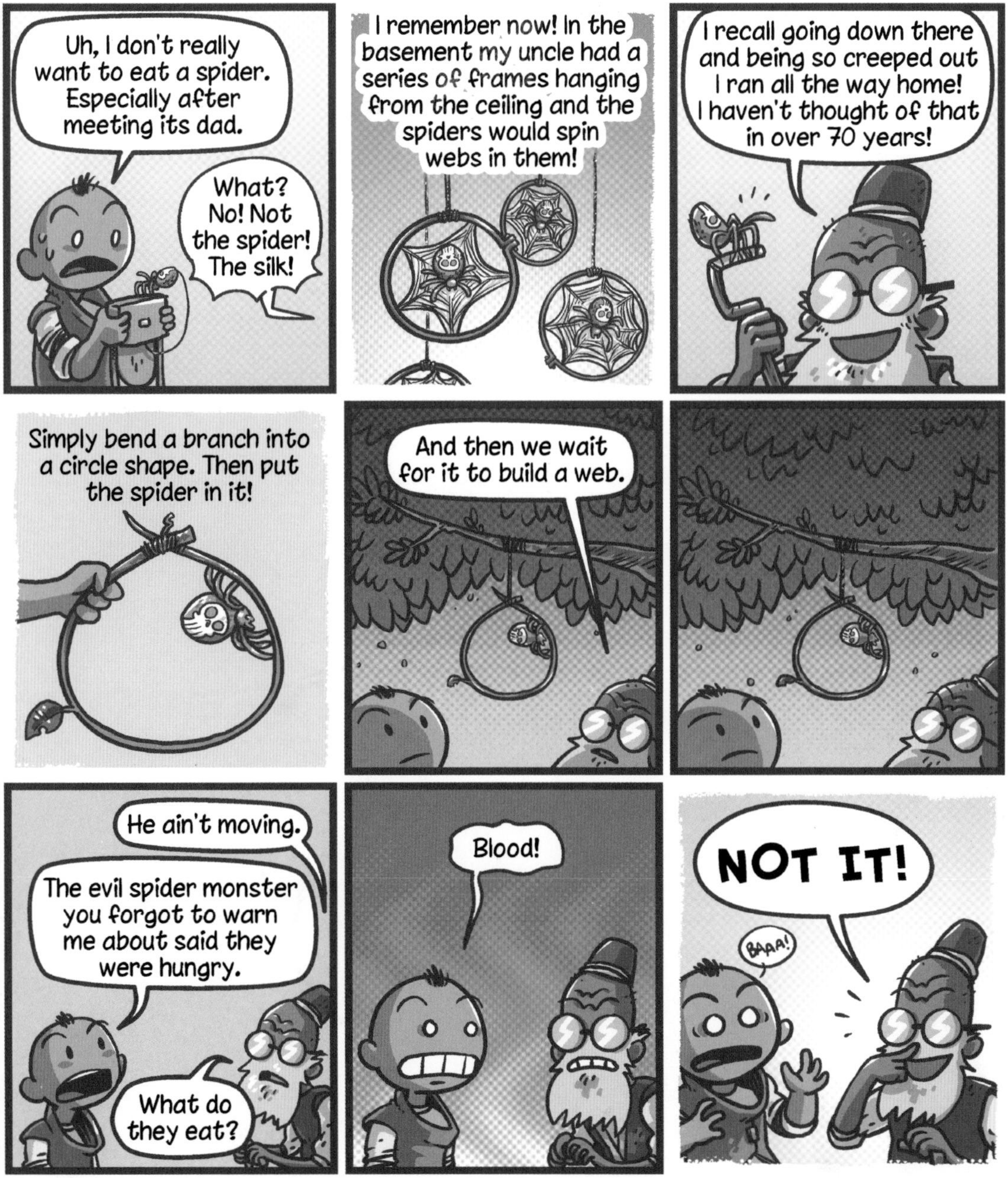
Uh, I don't really want to eat a spider. Especially after meeting its dad.
What? No! Not the spider! The silk!
I remember now! In the basement my uncle had a series of frames hanging from the ceiling and the spiders would spin webs in them!
I recall going down there and being so creeped out I ran all the way home! I haven't thought of that in over 70 years!
Simply bend a branch into a circle shape. Then put the spider in it!
And then we wait for it to build a web.
He ain't moving.
The evil spider monster you forgot to warn me about said they were hungry.
What do they eat?
Blood!
NOT IT!
BAAA!

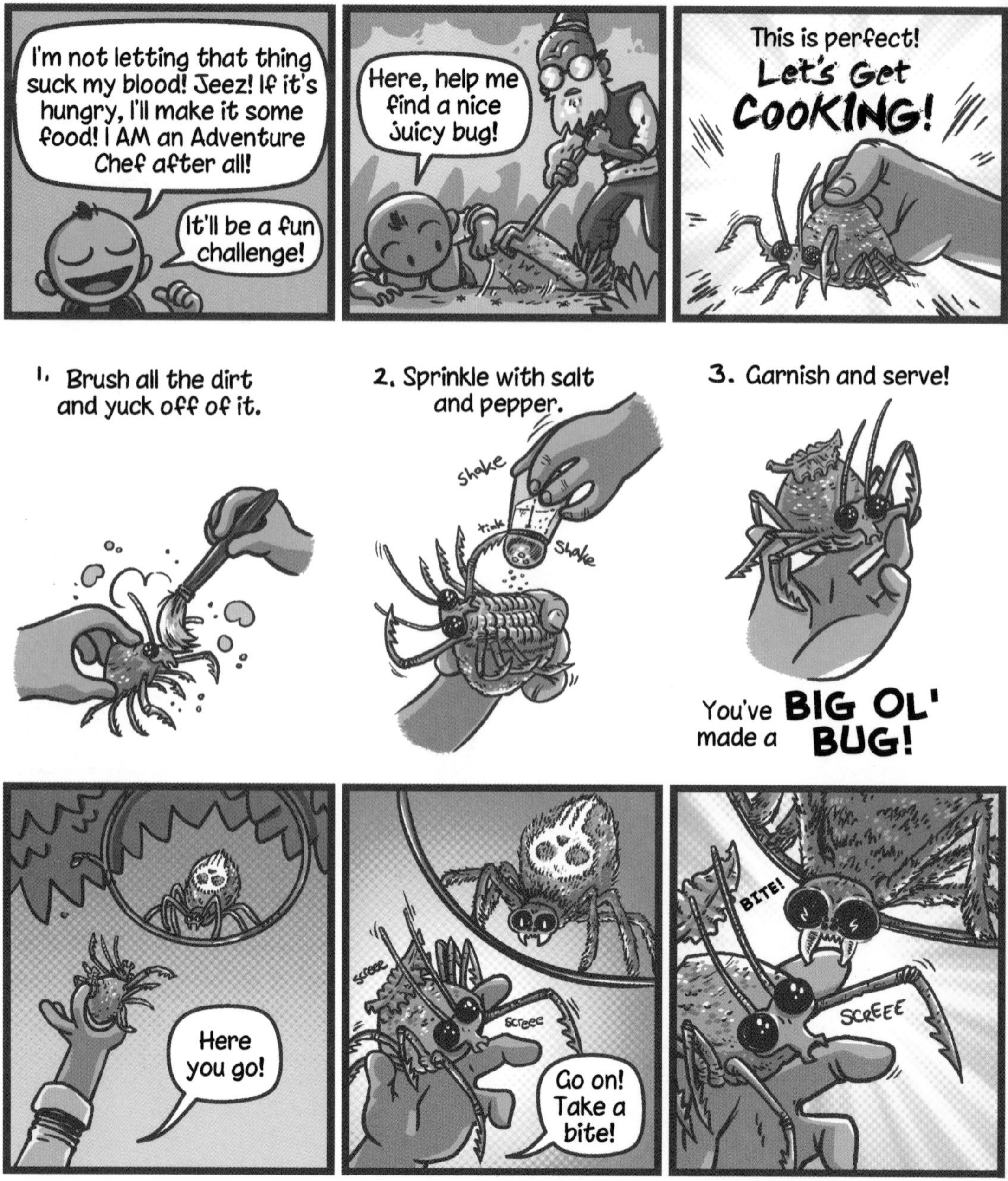
I'm not letting that thing suck my blood! Jeez! If it's hungry, I'll make it some food! I AM an Adventure Chef after all!
It'll be a fun challenge!
Here, help me find a nice juicy bug!
This is perfect!
Let's Get COOKING!
1. Brush all the dirt and yuck off of it.
2. Sprinkle with salt and pepper.
shake
tink
shake
3. Garnish and serve!
You've made a BIG OL' BUG!
Here you go!
screee
screee
Go on! Take a bite!
BITE!
SCREEE

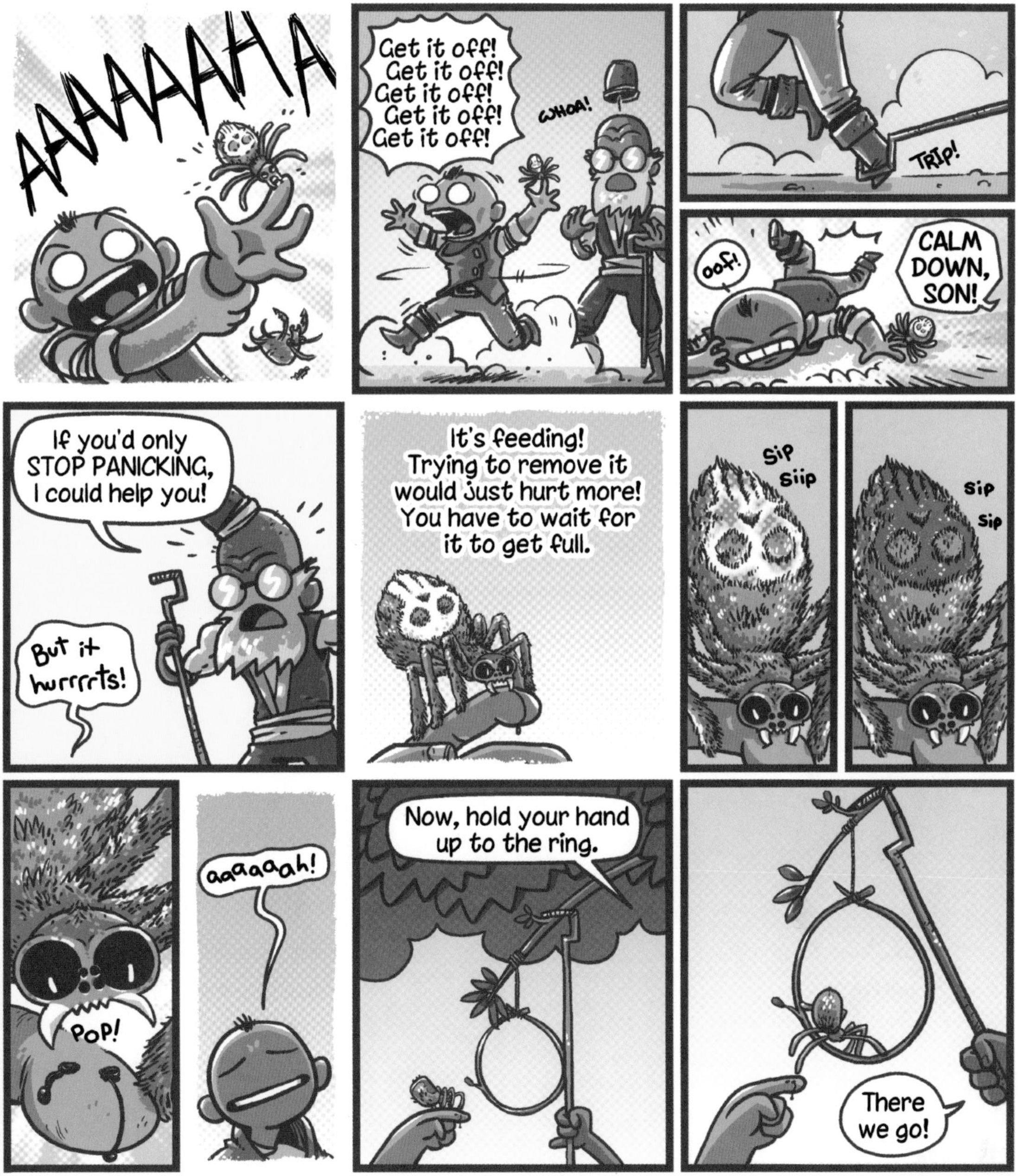
AAAAAAAHA
Get it off! Get it off! Get it off! Get it off! Get it off!
WHOA!
TRIP!
oof!
CALM DOWN, SON!
If you'd only STOP PANICKING, I could help you!
But it hurrrrts!
It's feeding! Trying to remove it would just hurt more! You have to wait for it to get full.
Sip
Siip
Sip
Sip
POP!
aaaaaah!
Now, hold your hand up to the ring.
There we go!

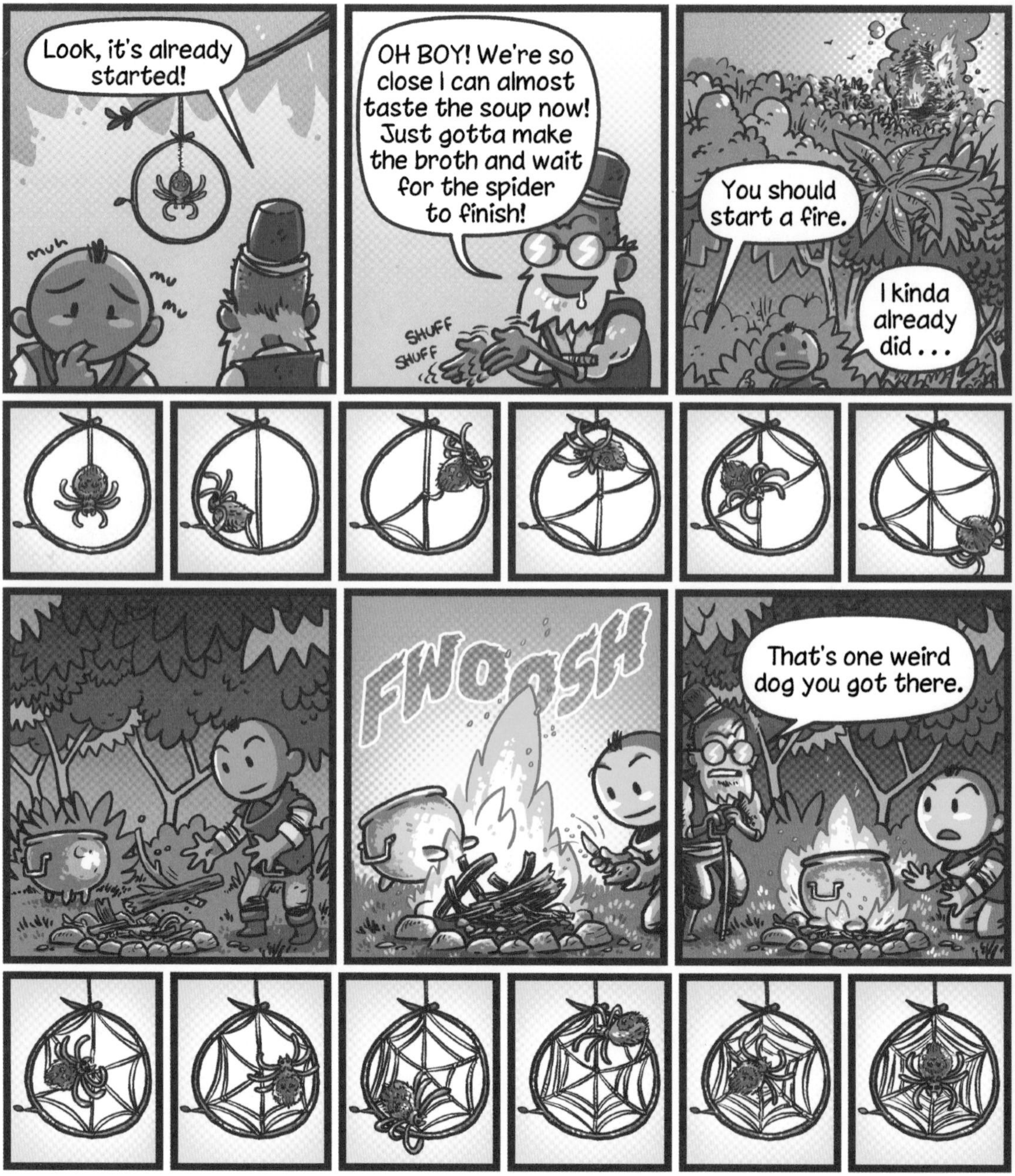
Look, it's already started!
muh
mu
mu
OH BOY! We're so close I can almost taste the soup now! Just gotta make the broth and wait for the spider to finish!
SHUFF
SHUFF
You should start a fire.
I kinda already did . . .
FWOOSH
That's one weird dog you got there.

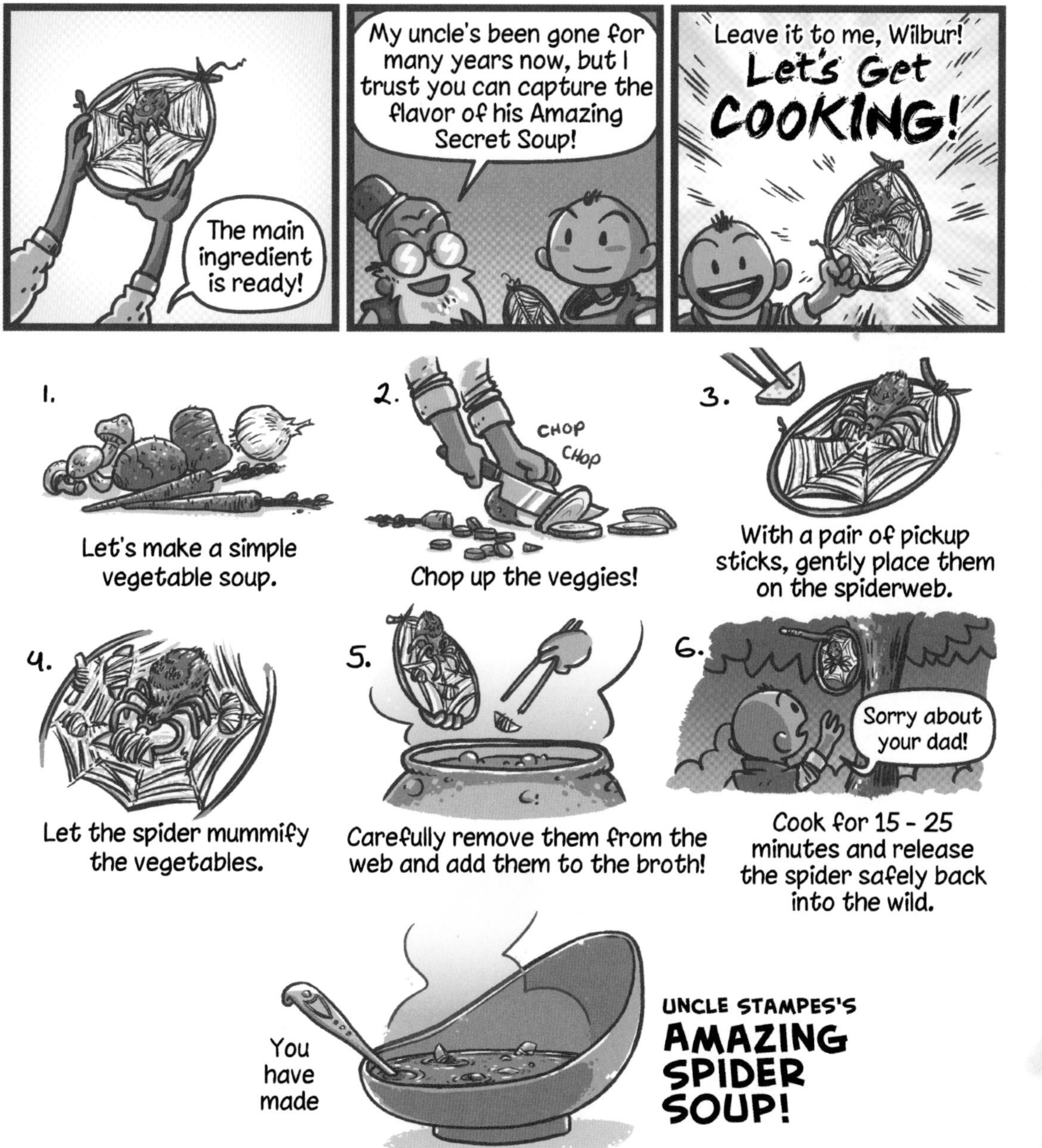
The main ingredient is ready!
My uncle's been gone for many years now, but I trust you can capture the flavor of his Amazing Secret Soup!
Leave it to me, Wilbur!
Let's Get COOKING!
1.
Let's make a simple vegetable soup.
2.
CHOP
CHOP
Chop up the veggies!
3.
With a pair of pickup sticks, gently place them on the spiderweb.
4.
Let the spider mummify the vegetables.
5.
Carefully remove them from the web and add them to the broth!
6.
Sorry about your dad!
Cook for 15 - 25 minutes and release the spider safely back into the wild.
You have made
UNCLE STAMPES'S
AMAZING SPIDER SOUP!

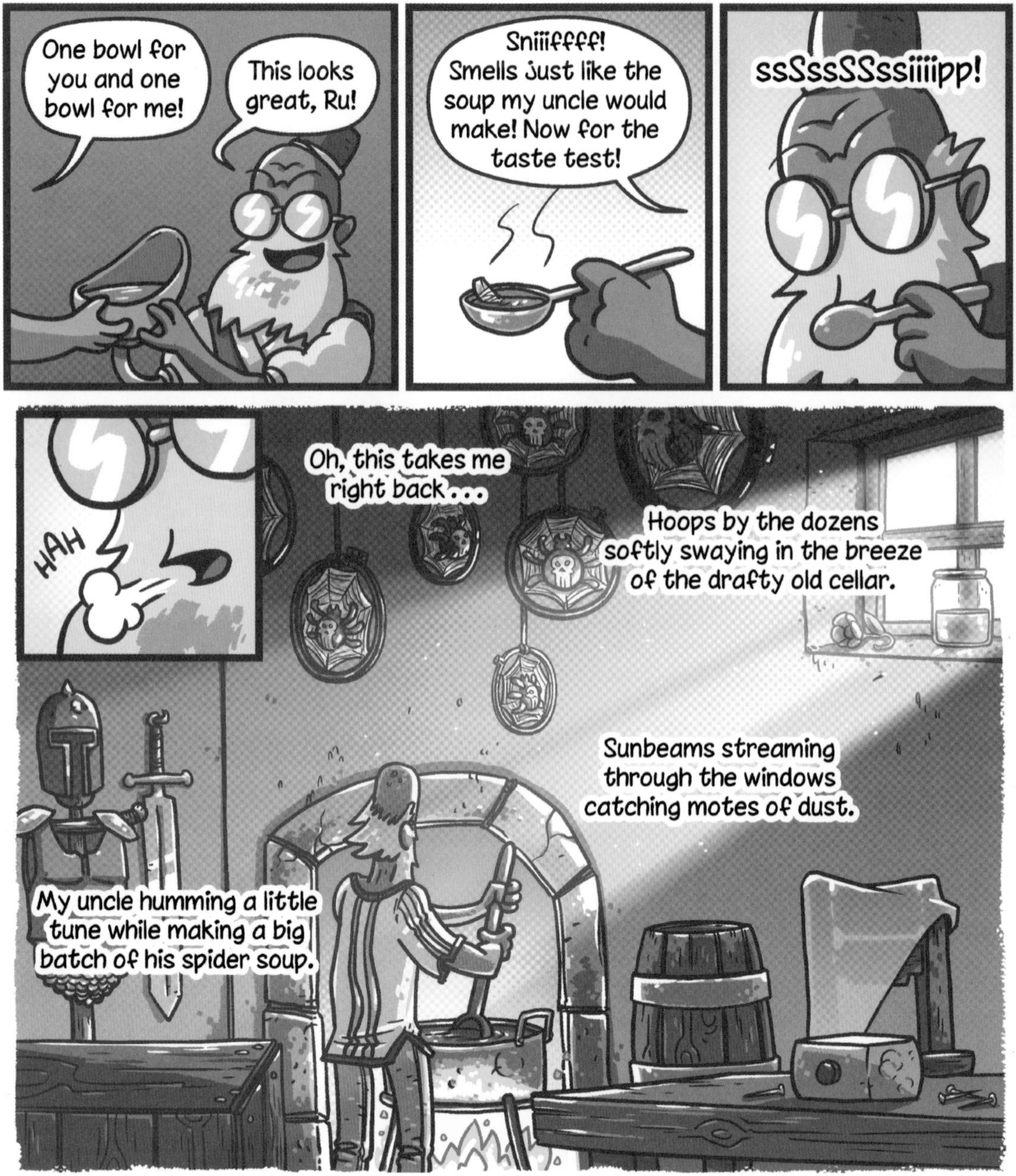
One bowl for you and one bowl for me!
This looks great, Ru!
Sniiiffff! Smells just like the soup my uncle would make! Now for the taste test!
ssSssSSssiiiipp!
HAH
Oh, this takes me right back . . .
Hoops by the dozens softly swaying in the breeze of the drafty old cellar.
Sunbeams streaming through the windows catching motes of dust.
My uncle humming a little tune while making a big batch of his spider soup.

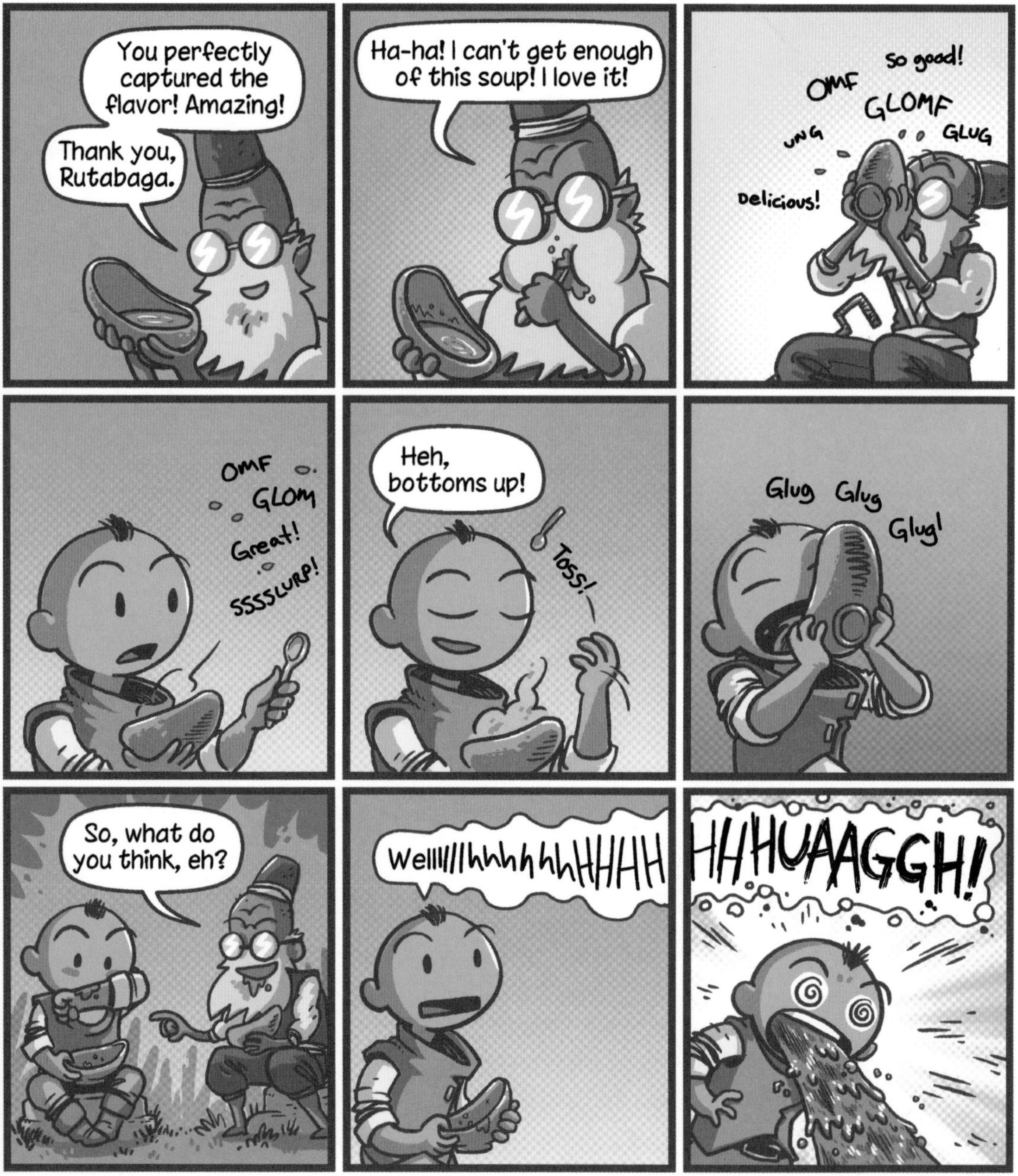
You perfectly captured the flavor! Amazing!
Thank you, Rutabaga.
Ha-ha! I can't get enough of this soup! I love it!
OMF
So good!
GLOMF
UNG
GLUG
Delicious!
OMF
GLOM
Great!
SSSSLURP!
Heh, bottoms up!
Toss!
Glug Glug Glug!
So, what do you think, eh?
WellllllhhhhhhHHHH
HHHUAAGGH!

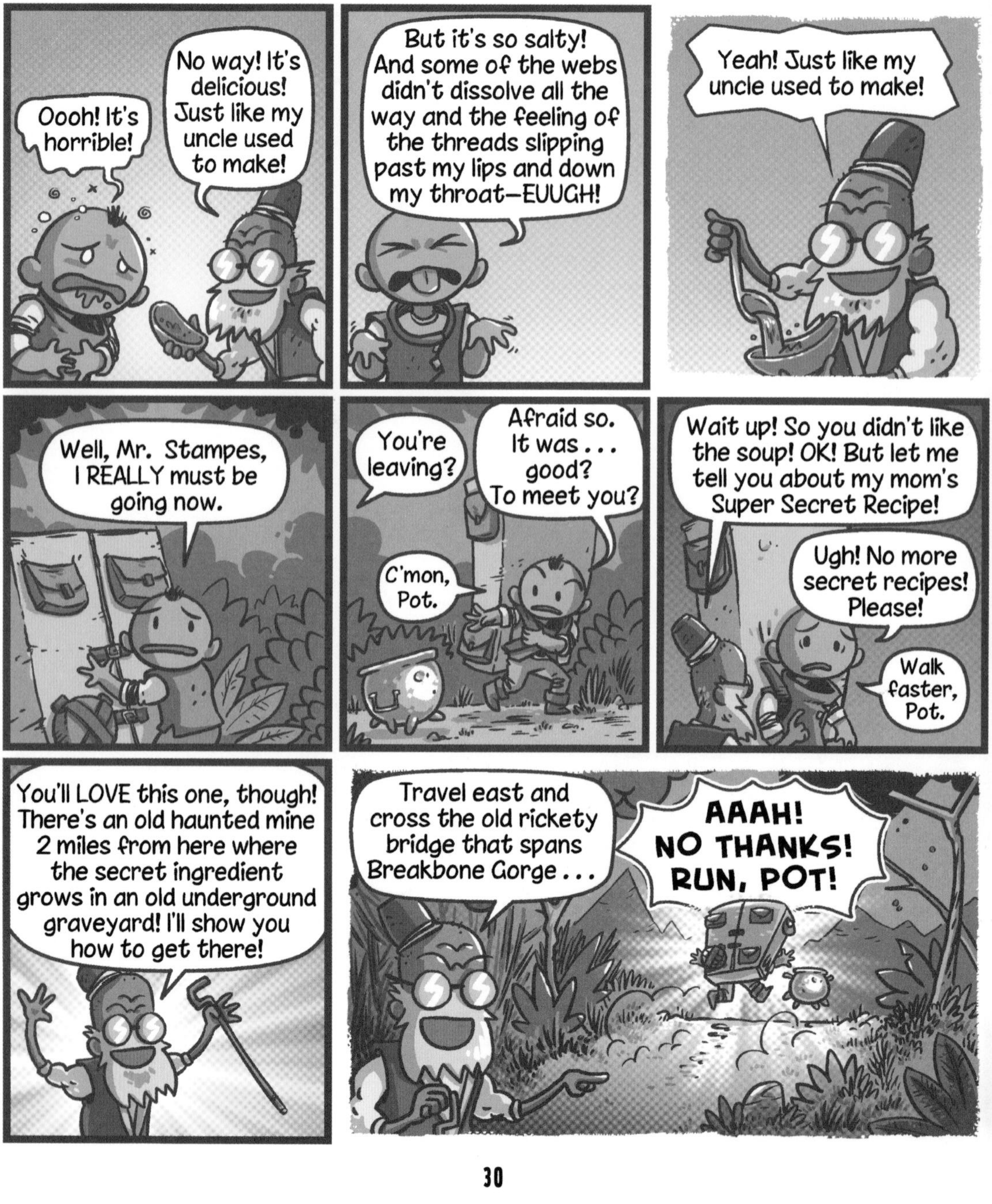
Oooh! It's horrible!
No way! It's delicious! Just like my uncle used to make!
But it's so salty! And some of the webs didn't dissolve all the way and the feeling of the threads slipping past my lips and down my throat—EUUGH!
Yeah! Just like my uncle used to make!
Well, Mr. Stampes, I REALLY must be going now.
You're leaving?
Afraid so. It was . . . good? To meet you?
C'mon, Pot.
Wait up! So you didn't like the soup! OK! But let me tell you about my mom's Super Secret Recipe!
Ugh! No more secret recipes! Please!
Walk faster, Pot.
You'll LOVE this one, though! There's an old haunted mine 2 miles from here where the secret ingredient grows in an old underground graveyard! I'll show you how to get there!
Travel east and cross the old rickety bridge that spans Breakbone Gorge . . .
AAAH! NO THANKS! RUN, POT!

END OF
CHAPTER ONE

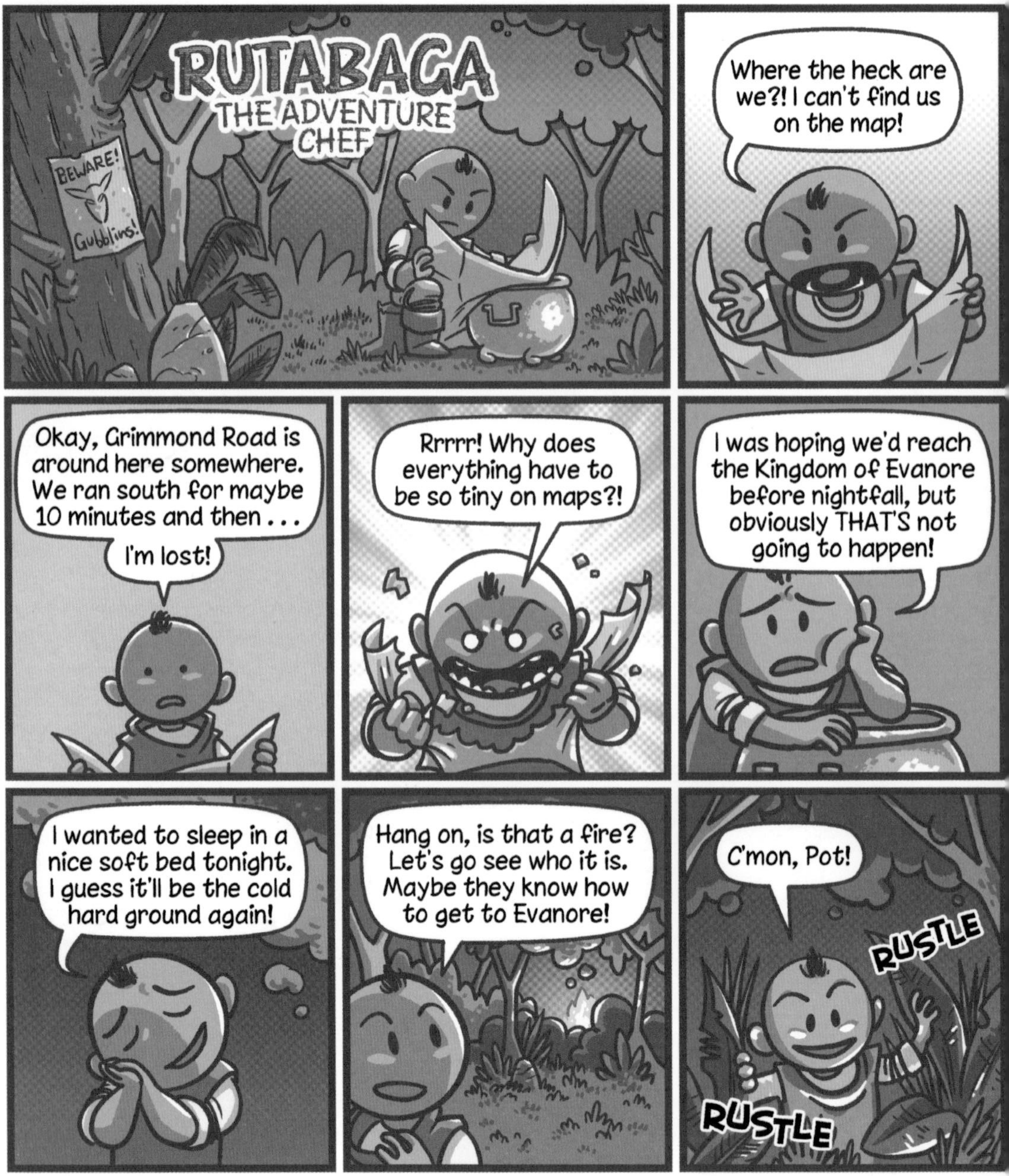
RUTABAGA
THE ADVENTURE CHEF
BEWARE!
Gubblins!
Where the heck are we?! I can't find us on the map!
Okay, Grimmond Road is around here somewhere. We ran south for maybe 10 minutes and then . . .
I'm lost!
Rrrrr! Why does everything have to be so tiny on maps?!
I was hoping we'd reach the Kingdom of Evanore before nightfall, but obviously THAT'S not going to happen!
I wanted to sleep in a nice soft bed tonight. I guess it'll be the cold hard ground again!
Hang on, is that a fire? Let's go see who it is. Maybe they know how to get to Evanore!
C'mon, Pot!
RUSTLE
RUSTLE

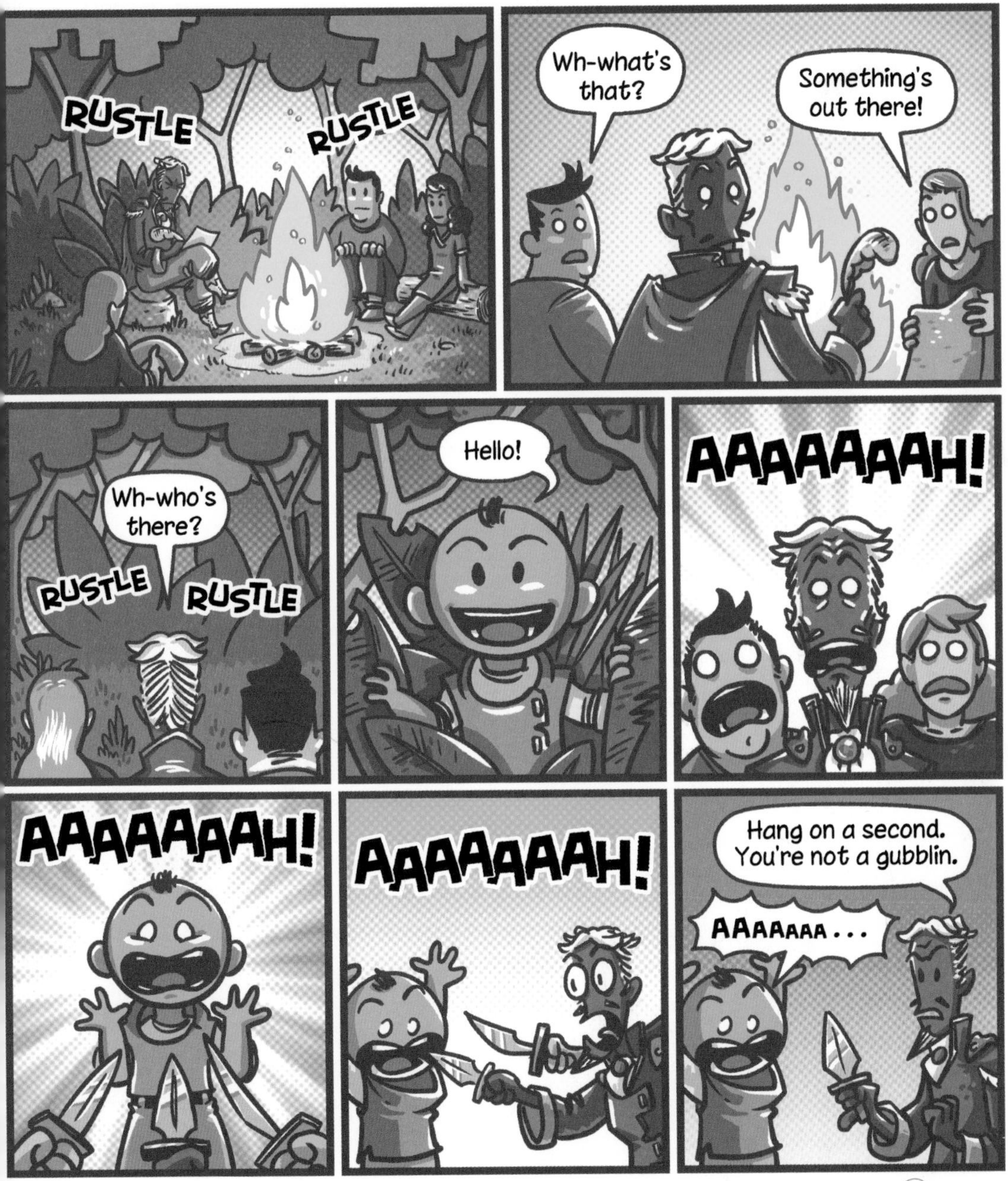
RUSTLE
RUSTLE
Wh-what's that?
Something's out there!
Wh-who's there?
RUSTLE
RUSTLE
Hello!
AAAAAAAH!
AAAAAAAH!
AAAAAAAH!
Hang on a second. You're not a gubblin.
AAAAAAA...

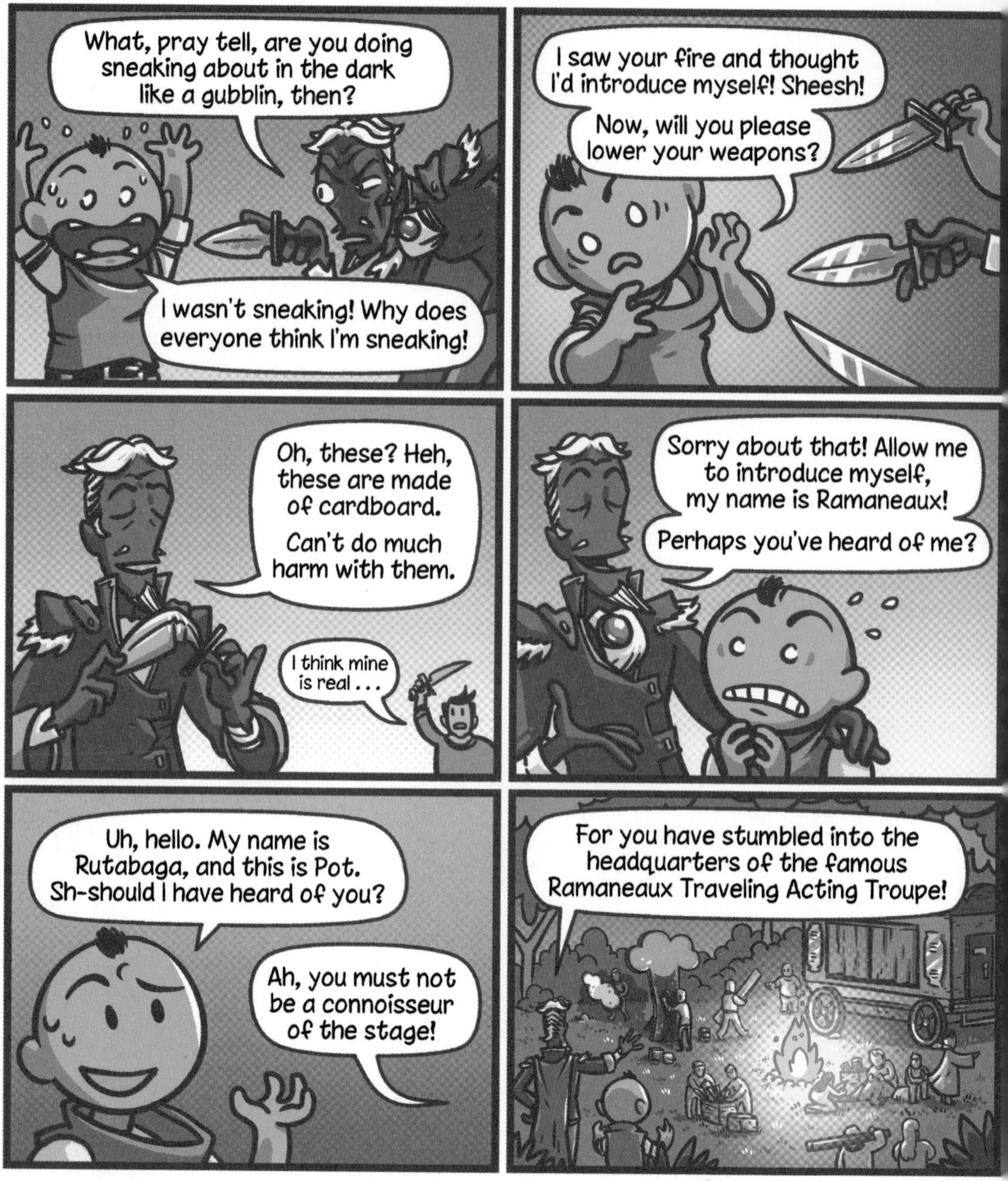
What, pray tell, are you doing sneaking about in the dark like a gubblin, then?
I wasn't sneaking! Why does everyone think I'm sneaking!
I saw your fire and thought I'd introduce myself! Sheesh!
Now, will you please lower your weapons?
Oh, these? Heh, these are made of cardboard.
Can't do much harm with them.
I think mine is real . . .
Sorry about that! Allow me to introduce myself, my name is Ramaneaux!
Perhaps you've heard of me?
Uh, hello. My name is Rutabaga, and this is Pot. Sh-should I have heard of you?
Ah, you must not be a connoisseur of the stage!
For you have stumbled into the headquarters of the famous Ramaneaux Traveling Acting Troupe!

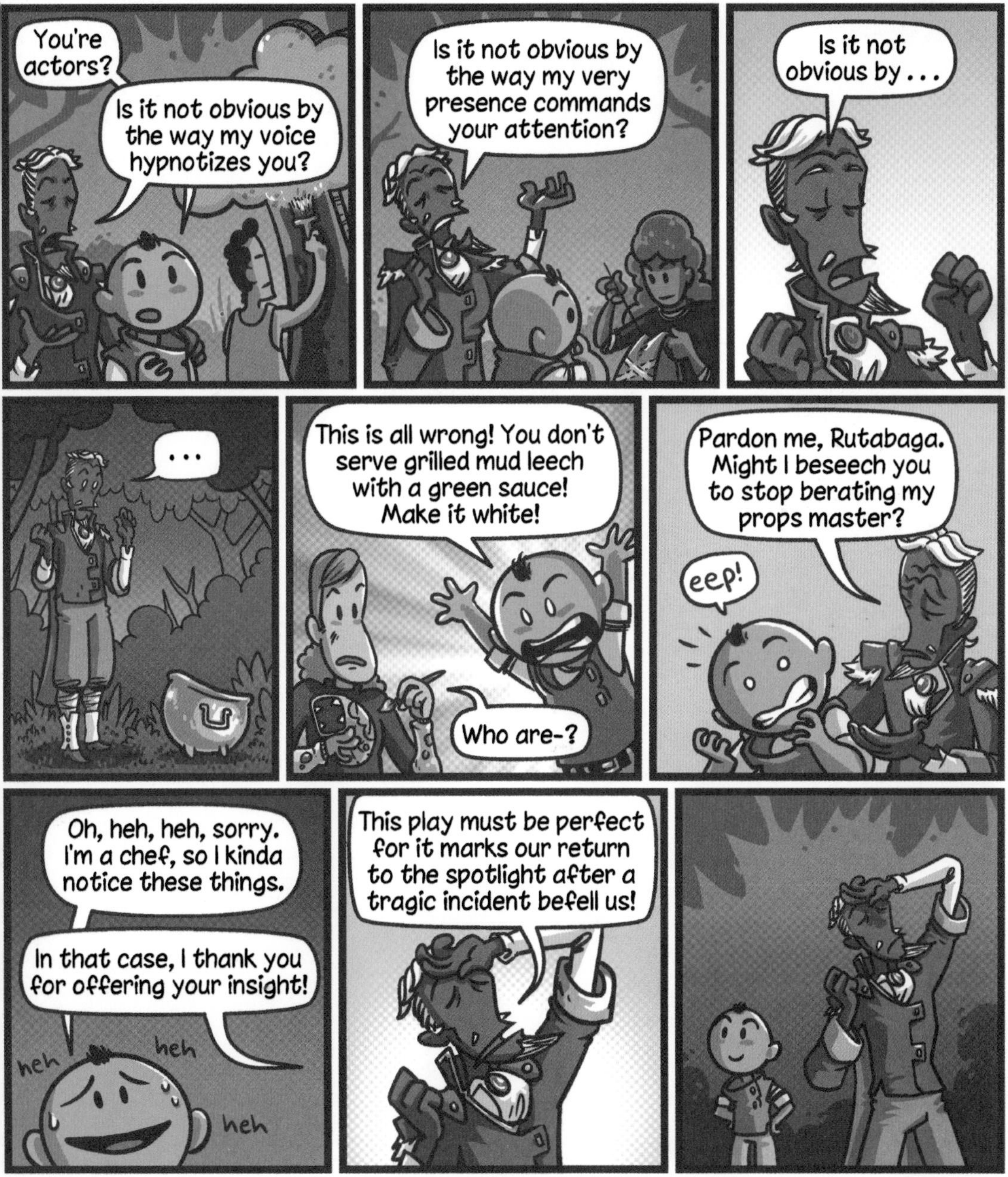
You're actors?
Is it not obvious by the way my voice hypnotizes you?
Is it not obvious by the way my very presence commands your attention?
Is it not obvious by . . .
. . .
This is all wrong! You don't serve grilled mud leech with a green sauce! Make it white!
Who are-?
Pardon me, Rutabaga. Might I beseech you to stop berating my props master?
eep!
Oh, heh, heh, sorry. I'm a chef, so I kinda notice these things.
In that case, I thank you for offering your insight!
heh
heh
heh
This play must be perfect for it marks our return to the spotlight after a tragic incident befell us!

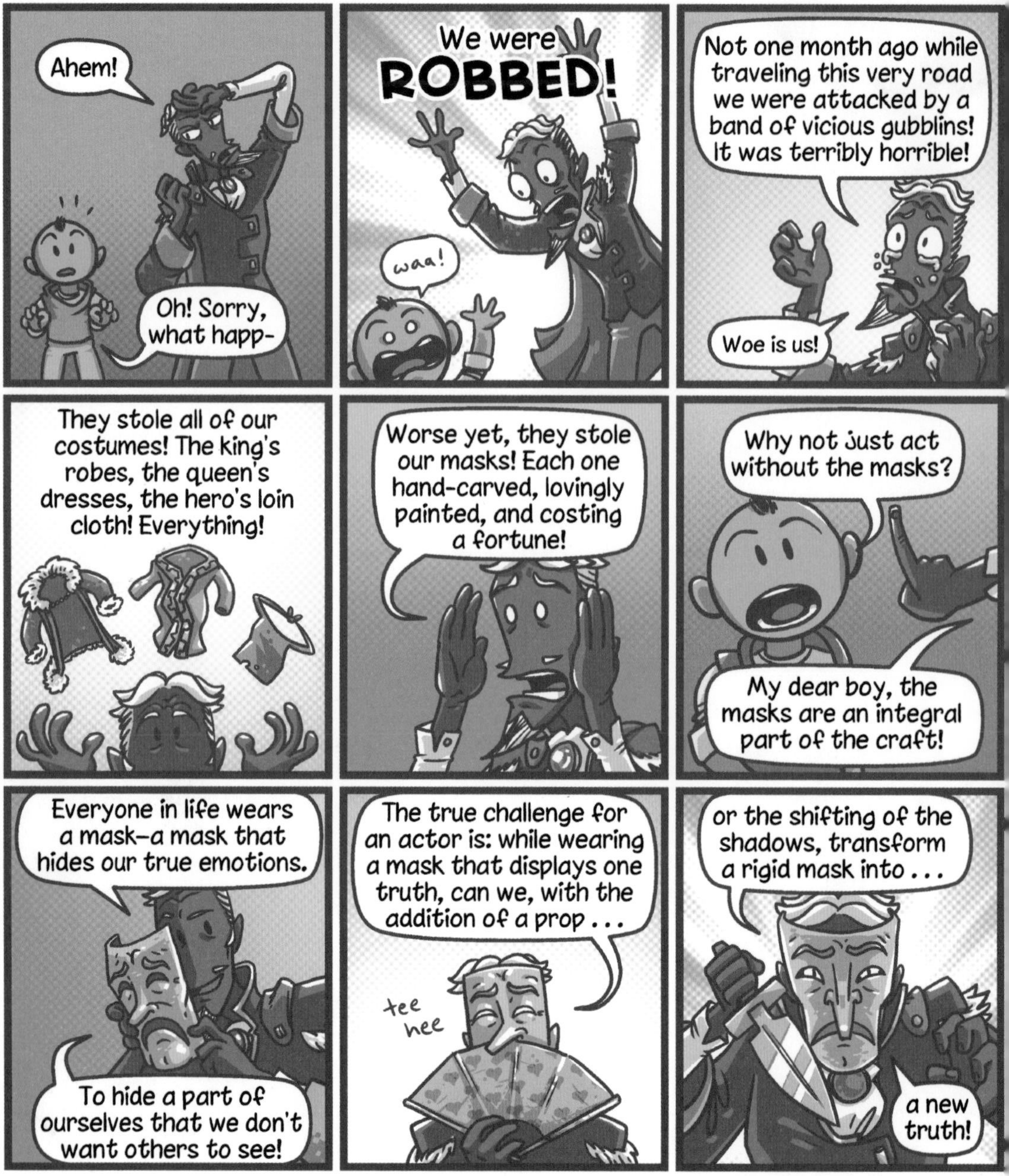
Ahem!
Oh! Sorry, what happ-
We were ROBBED!
waa!
Not one month ago while traveling this very road we were attacked by a band of vicious gubblins! It was terribly horrible!
Woe is us!
They stole all of our costumes! The king's robes, the queen's dresses, the hero's loin cloth! Everything!
Worse yet, they stole our masks! Each one hand-carved, lovingly painted, and costing a fortune!
Why not just act without the masks?
My dear boy, the masks are an integral part of the craft!
Everyone in life wears a mask—a mask that hides our true emotions.
To hide a part of ourselves that we don't want others to see!
The true challenge for an actor is: while wearing a mask that displays one truth, can we, with the addition of a prop . . .
tee hee
or the shifting of the shadows, transform a rigid mask into . . .
a new truth!

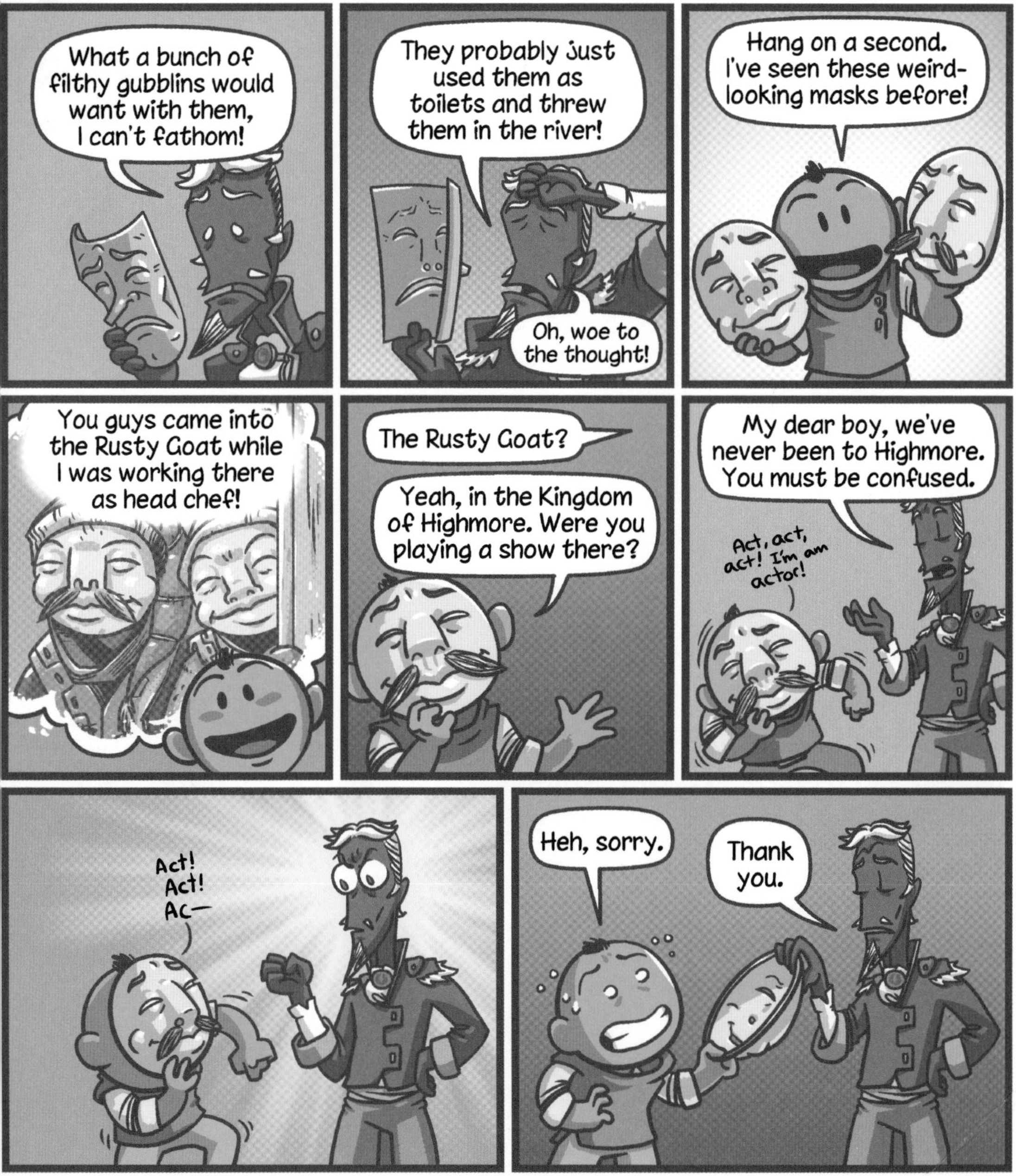
What a bunch of filthy gubblins would want with them, I can't fathom!
They probably just used them as toilets and threw them in the river!
Oh, woe to the thought!
Hang on a second. I've seen these weird-looking masks before!
You guys came into the Rusty Goat while I was working there as head chef!
The Rusty Goat?
Yeah, in the Kingdom of Highmore. Were you playing a show there?
My dear boy, we've never been to Highmore. You must be confused.
Act, act, act! I'm an actor!
Act! Act! Ac—
Heh, sorry.
Thank you.

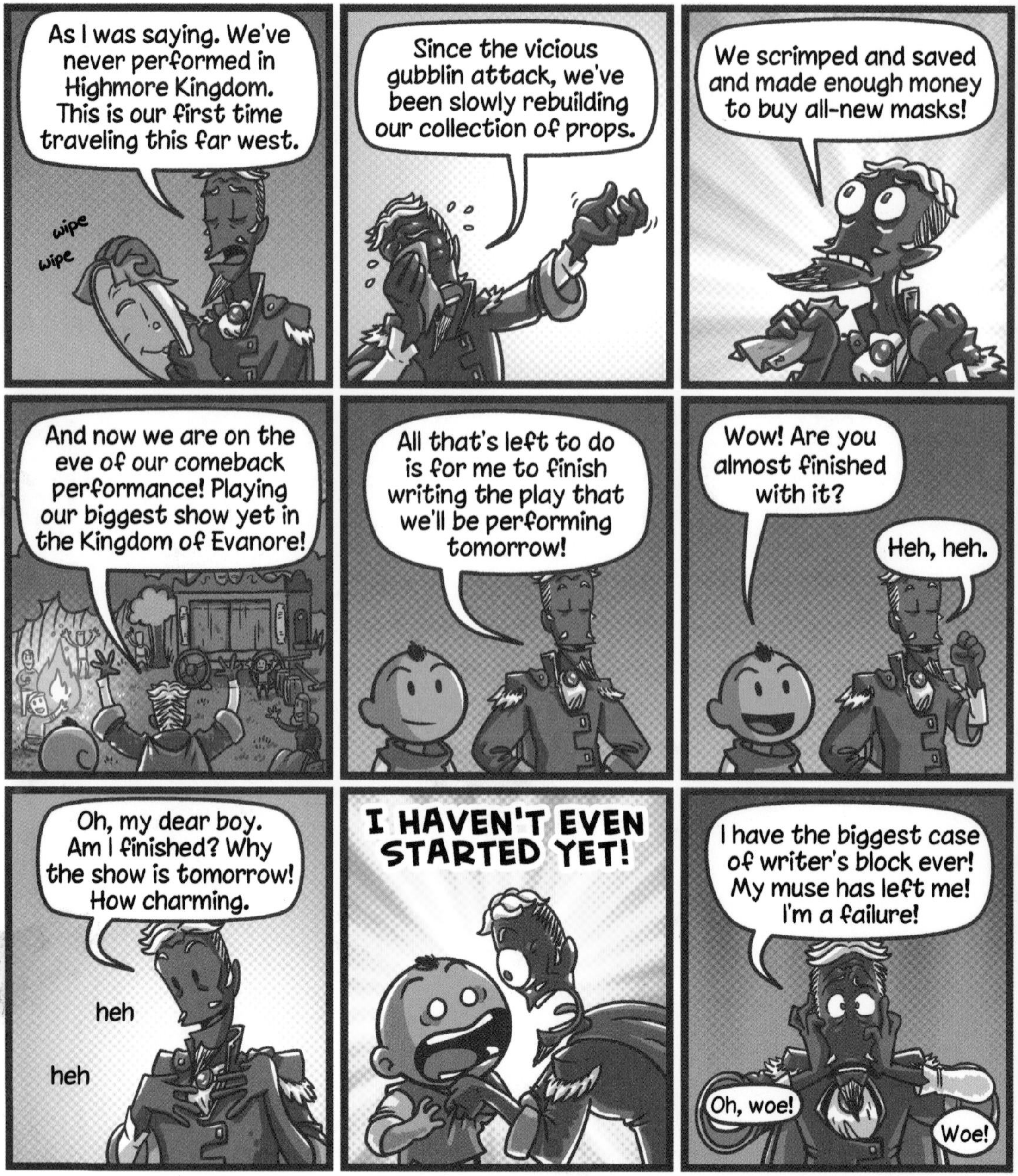
As I was saying. We've never performed in Highmore Kingdom. This is our first time traveling this far west.
wipe
wipe
Since the vicious gubblin attack, we've been slowly rebuilding our collection of props.
We scrimped and saved and made enough money to buy all-new masks!
And now we are on the eve of our comeback performance! Playing our biggest show yet in the Kingdom of Evanore!
All that's left to do is for me to finish writing the play that we'll be performing tomorrow!
Wow! Are you almost finished with it?
Heh, heh.
Oh, my dear boy. Am I finished? Why the show is tomorrow! How charming.
heh
heh
I HAVEN'T EVEN STARTED YET!
I have the biggest case of writer's block ever! My muse has left me! I'm a failure!
Oh, woe!
Woe!

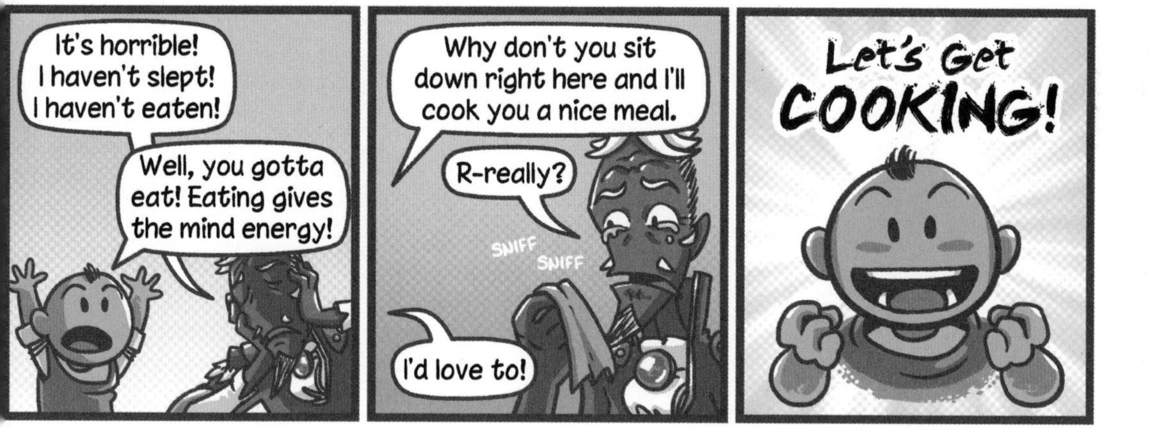
It's horrible! I haven't slept! I haven't eaten!
Well, you gotta eat! Eating gives the mind energy!
Why don't you sit down right here and I'll cook you a nice meal.
R-really?
SNIFF
SNIFF
I'd love to!
Let's Get COOKING!

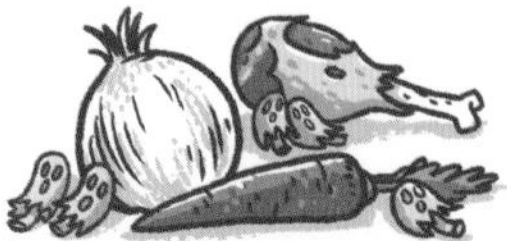

1. Gather shredded turkey, veggies, ghost mushrooms, chicken stock, and a single lime-green bean.

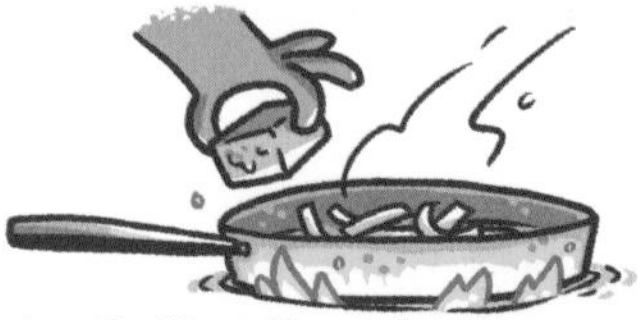

2. Soften the onion in a pan and add a whole heap of butter, flour, and the stock. Stir constantly until the sauce has thickened.

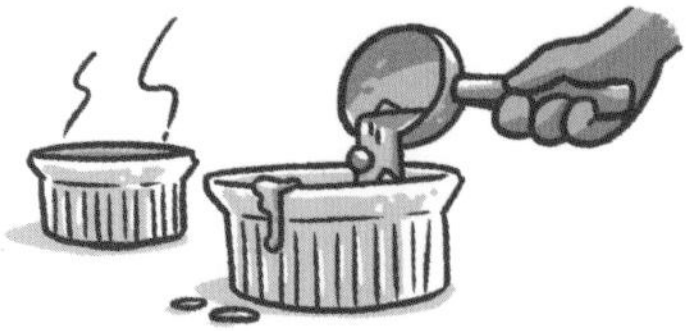

3. Add the rest of the ingredients and pour into individual bowls.

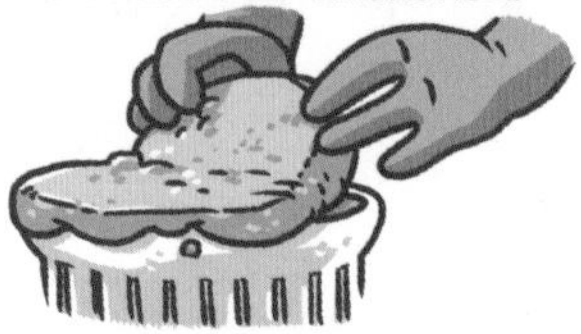

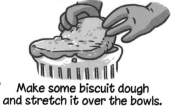

4. Make some biscuit dough and stretch it over the bowls.

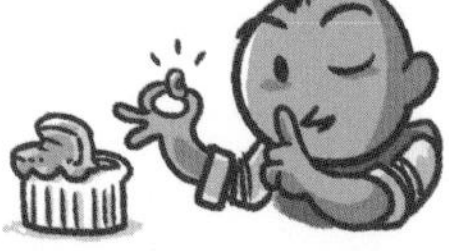

5. Choose one bowl and secretly drop the bean into it! Bake them all in an oven until the tops are golden brown!

You have made a

POISONED POT PIE

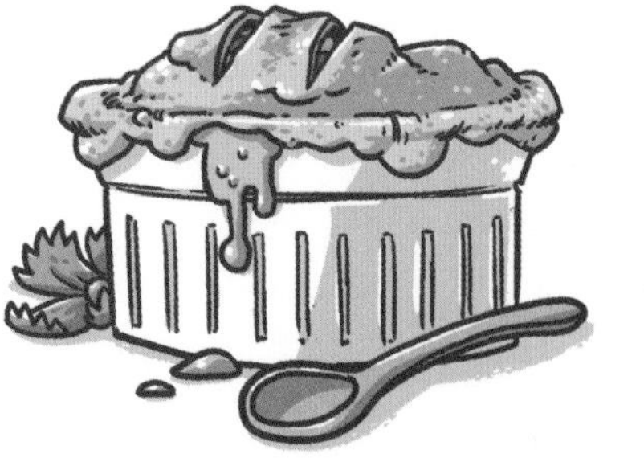

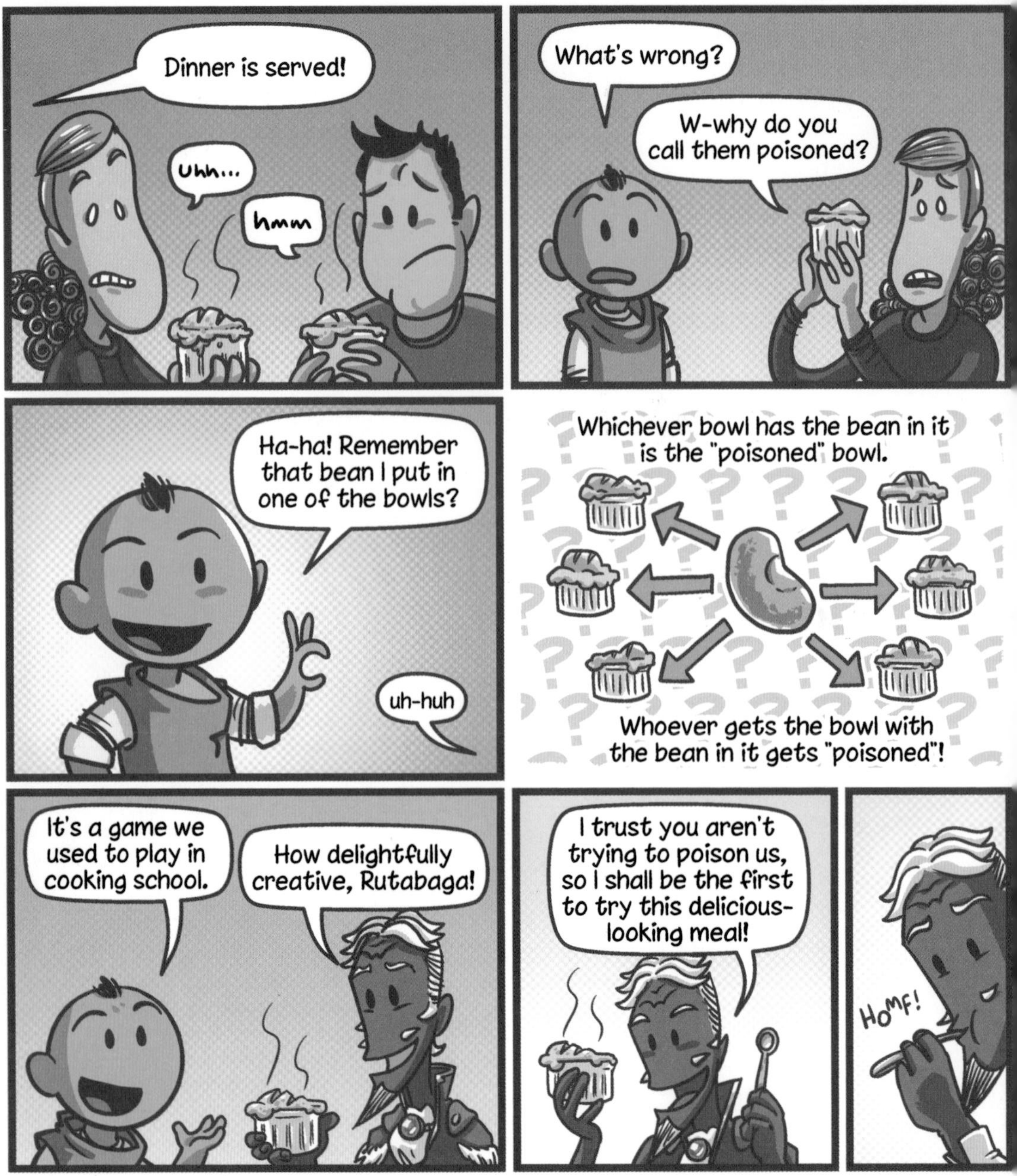
Dinner is served!
Uhh...
hmm
What's wrong?
W-why do you call them poisoned?
Ha-ha! Remember that bean I put in one of the bowls?
uh-huh
Whichever bowl has the bean in it is the "poisoned" bowl.
Whoever gets the bowl with the bean in it gets "poisoned"!
It's a game we used to play in cooking school.
How delightfully creative, Rutabaga!
I trust you aren't trying to poison us, so I shall be the first to try this delicious-looking meal!
HOMF!

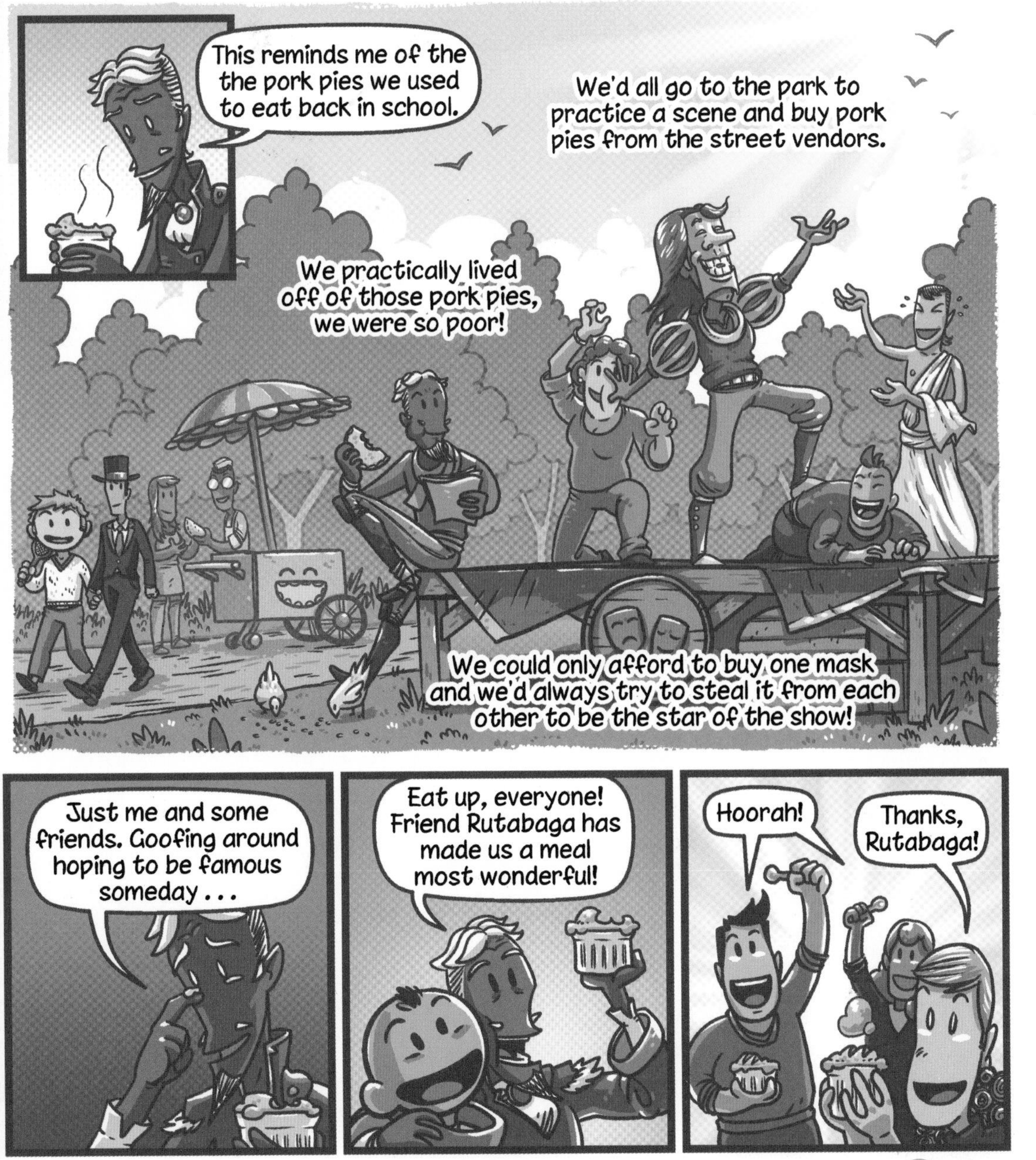
This reminds me of the the pork pies we used to eat back in school.
We'd all go to the park to practice a scene and buy pork pies from the street vendors.
We practically lived off of those pork pies, we were so poor!
We could only afford to buy one mask and we'd always try to steal it from each other to be the star of the show!
Just me and some friends. Goofing around hoping to be famous someday . . .
Eat up, everyone! Friend Rutabaga has made us a meal most wonderful!
Hoorah!
Thanks, Rutabaga!

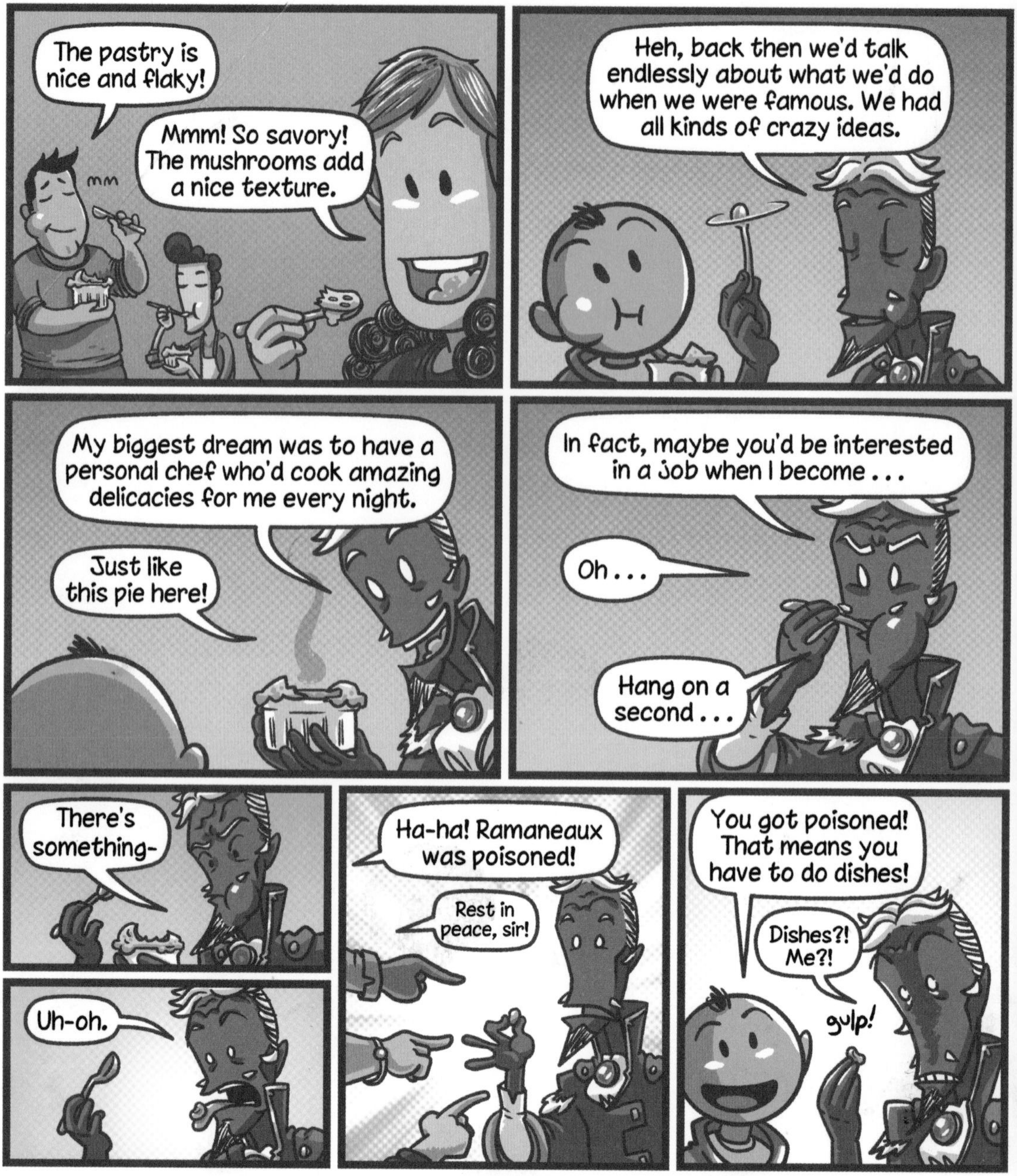
The pastry is nice and flaky!
mm
Mmm! So savory! The mushrooms add a nice texture.
Heh, back then we'd talk endlessly about what we'd do when we were famous. We had all kinds of crazy ideas.
My biggest dream was to have a personal chef who'd cook amazing delicacies for me every night.
Just like this pie here!
In fact, maybe you'd be interested in a job when I become . . .
Oh . . .
Hang on a second . . .
There's something-
Uh-oh.
Ha-ha! Ramaneaux was poisoned!
Rest in peace, sir!
You got poisoned! That means you have to do dishes!
Dishes?! Me?!
gulp!

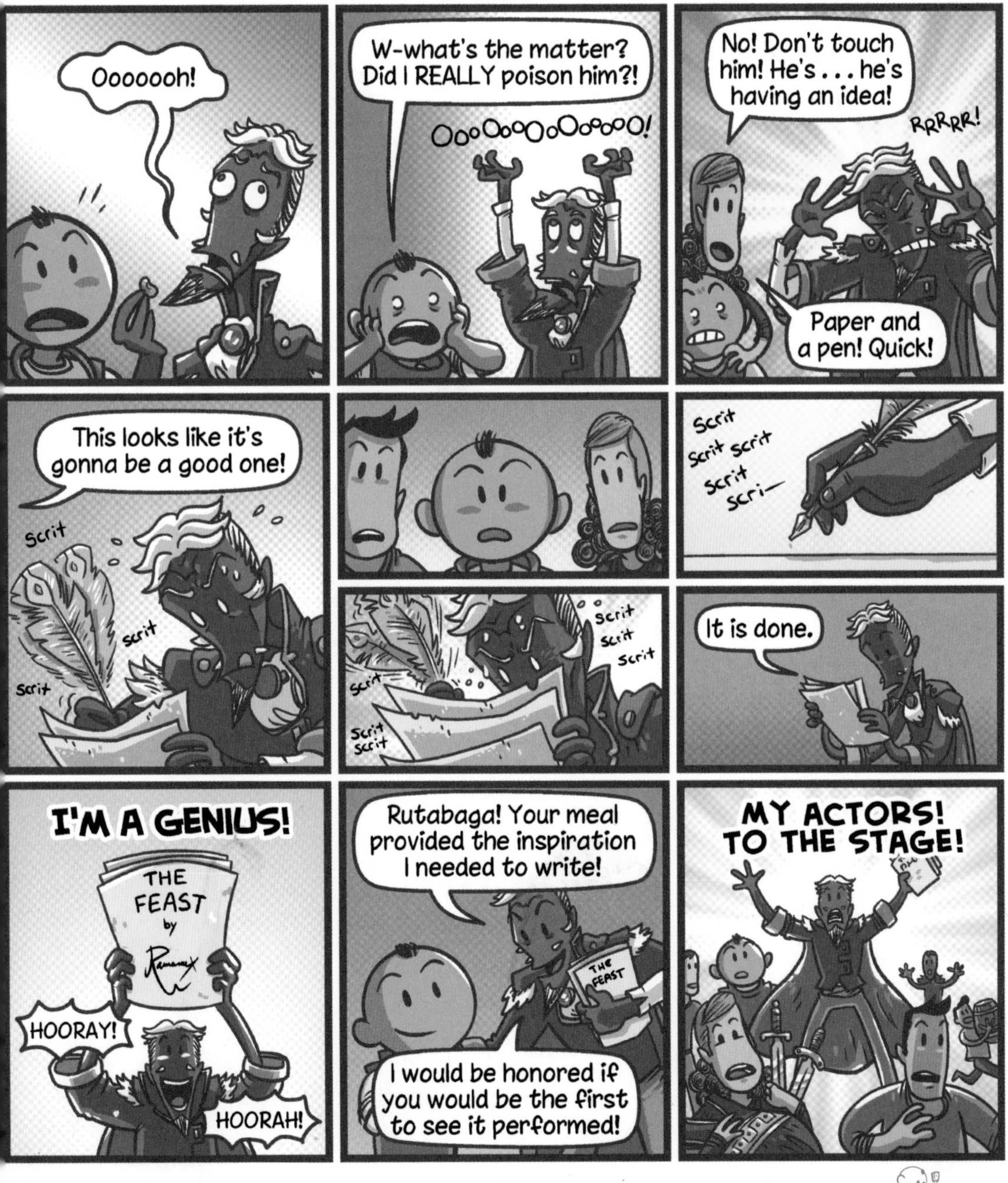
Ooooooh!
W-what's the matter? Did I REALLY poison him?!
OooOoOoOoOoOoO!
No! Don't touch him! He's . . . he's having an idea!
RRRRR!
Paper and a pen! Quick!
This looks like it's gonna be a good one!
Scrit
scrit
Scrit
Scrit
Scrit scrit
Scrit
Scri—
Scrit
Scrit
Scrit
Scrit
Scrit
Scrit
Scrit
It is done.
I'M A GENIUS!
THE FEAST by
HOORAY!
HOORAH!
Rutabaga! Your meal provided the inspiration I needed to write!
THE FEAST
I would be honored if you would be the first to see it performed!
MY ACTORS! TO THE STAGE!

44

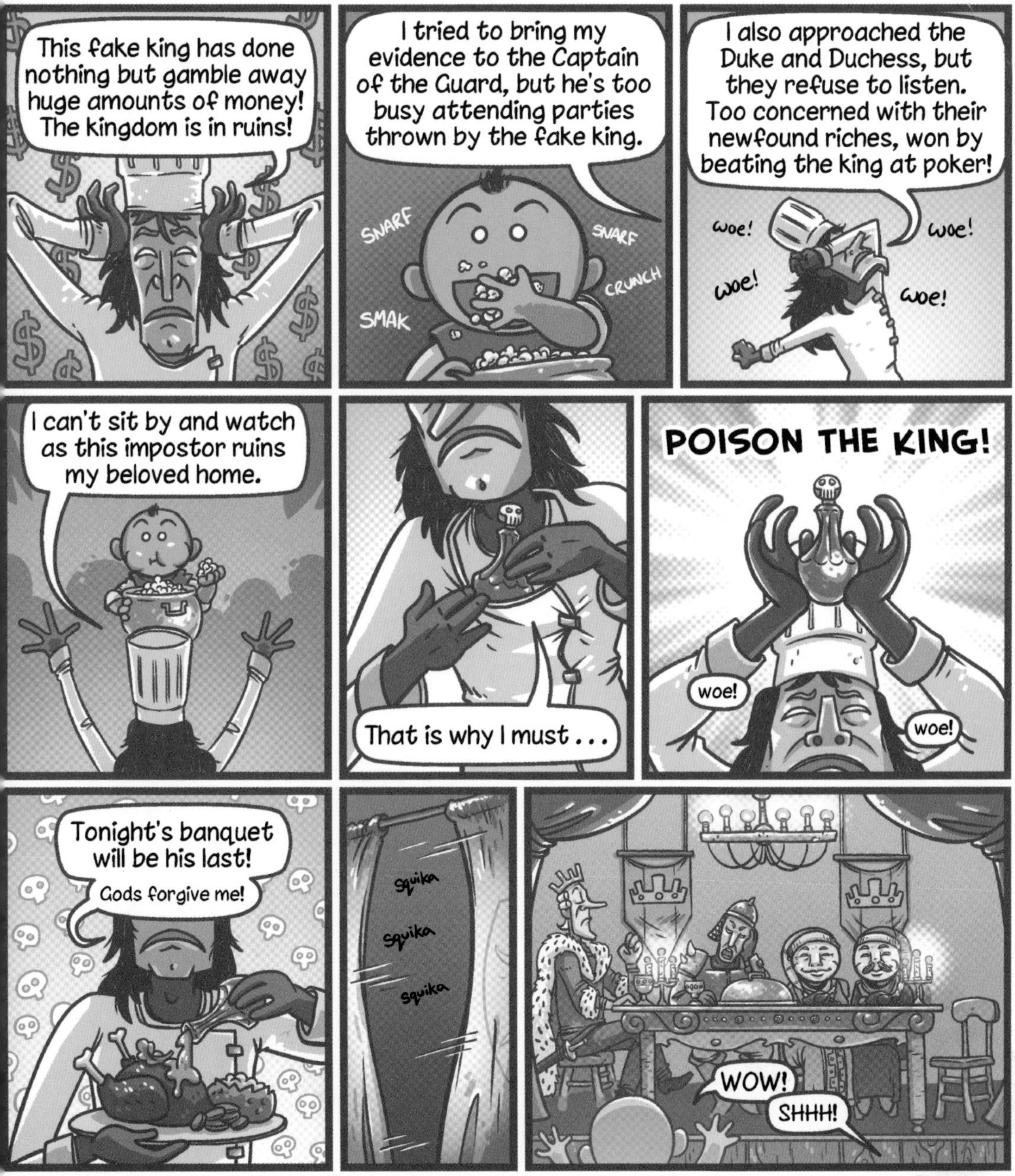
This fake king has done nothing but gamble away huge amounts of money! The kingdom is in ruins!
I tried to bring my evidence to the Captain of the Guard, but he's too busy attending parties thrown by the fake king.
SNARF
SNARF
CRUNCH
SMAK
I also approached the Duke and Duchess, but they refuse to listen. Too concerned with their newfound riches, won by beating the king at poker!
woe!
woe!
woe!
woe!
I can't sit by and watch as this impostor ruins my beloved home.
That is why I must . . .
POISON THE KING!
woe!
woe!
Tonight's banquet will be his last!
Gods forgive me!
squika
squika
squika
WOW!
SHHH!

47

End of Chapter Two

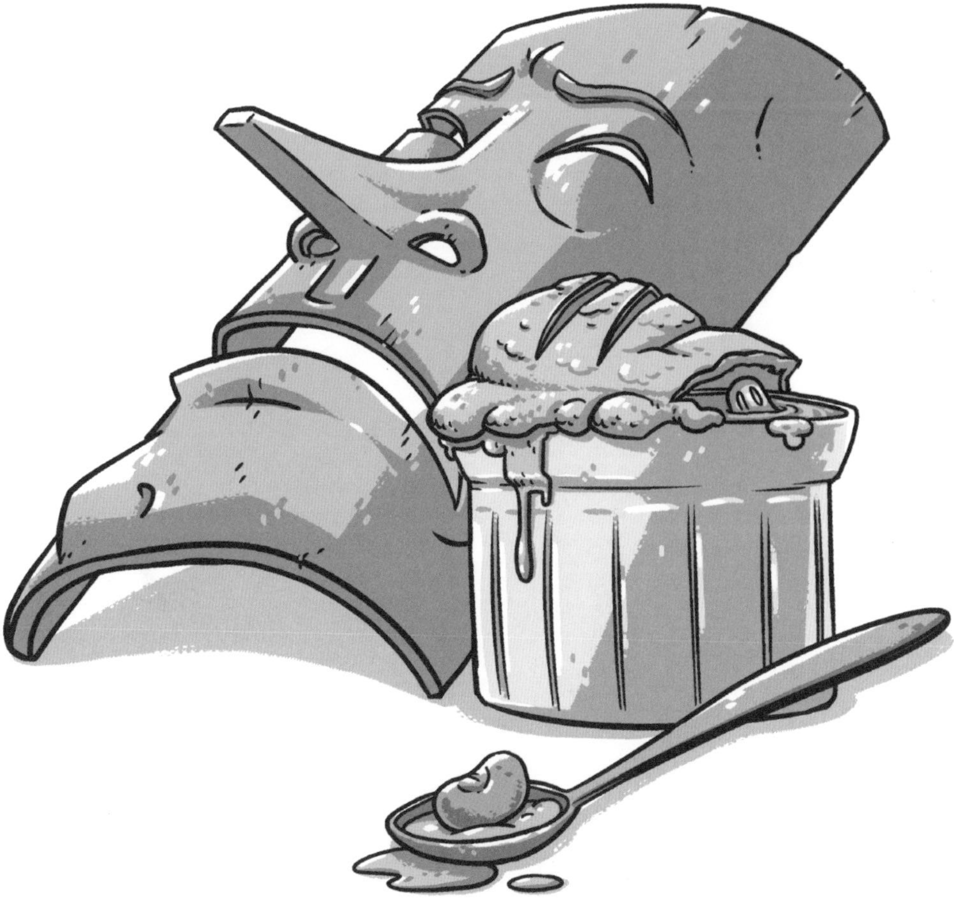

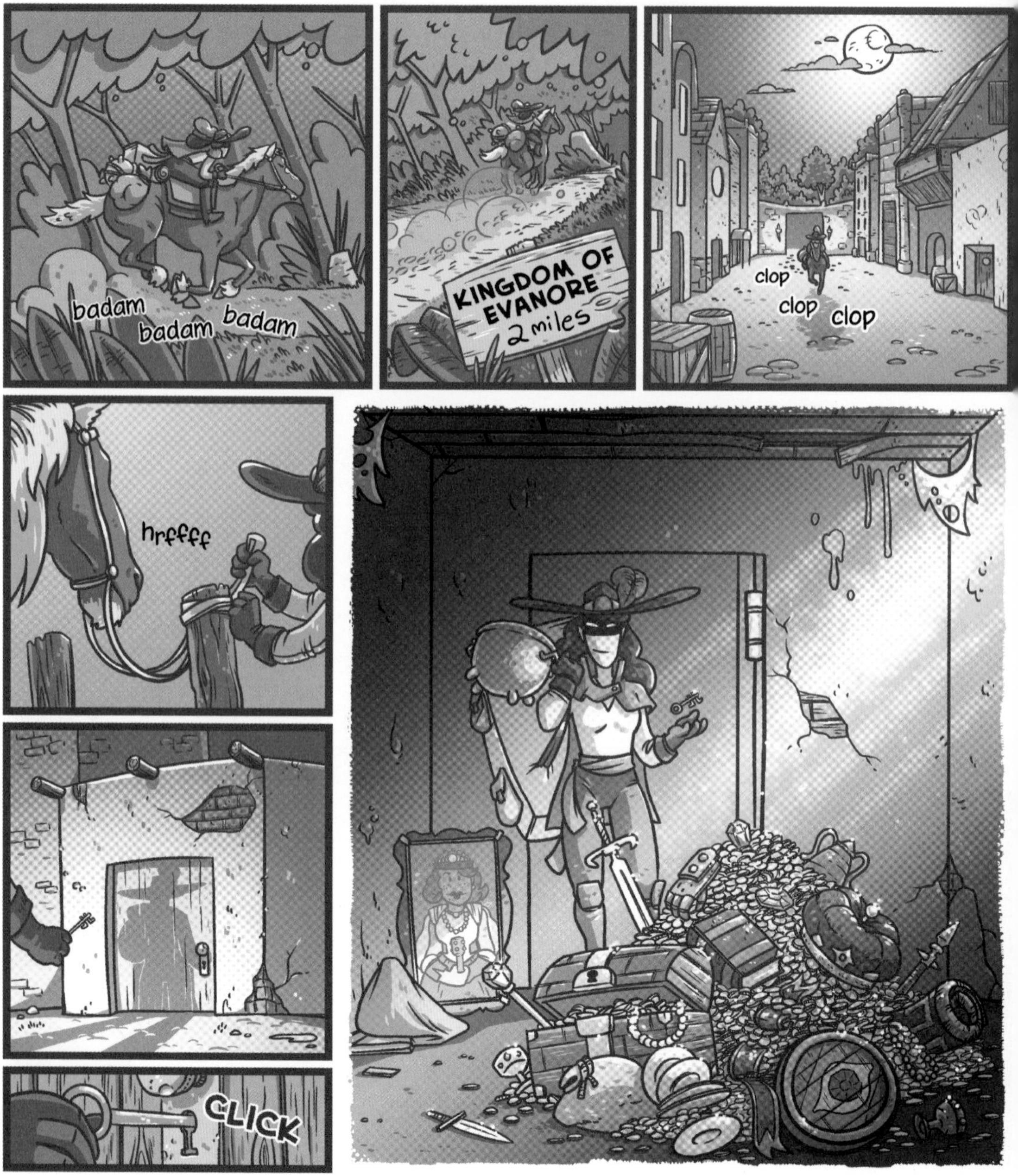
badam
badam
badam
KINGDOM OF EVANORE
2 miles
clop
clop
clop
hrffff
CLICK

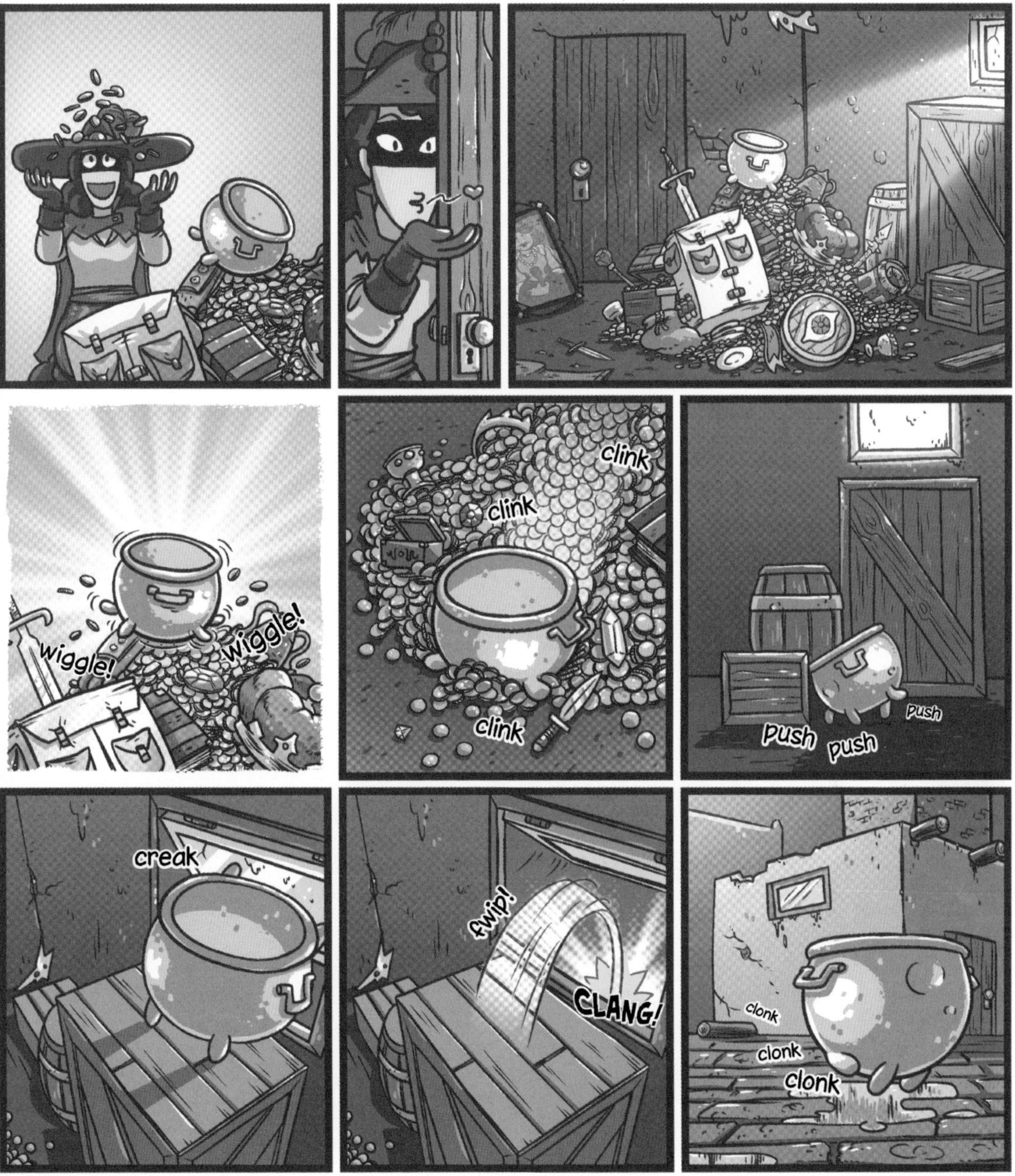
wiggle!
wiggle!
clink
clink
clink
push
push
push
creak
fwip!
CLANG!
clonk
clonk
clonk

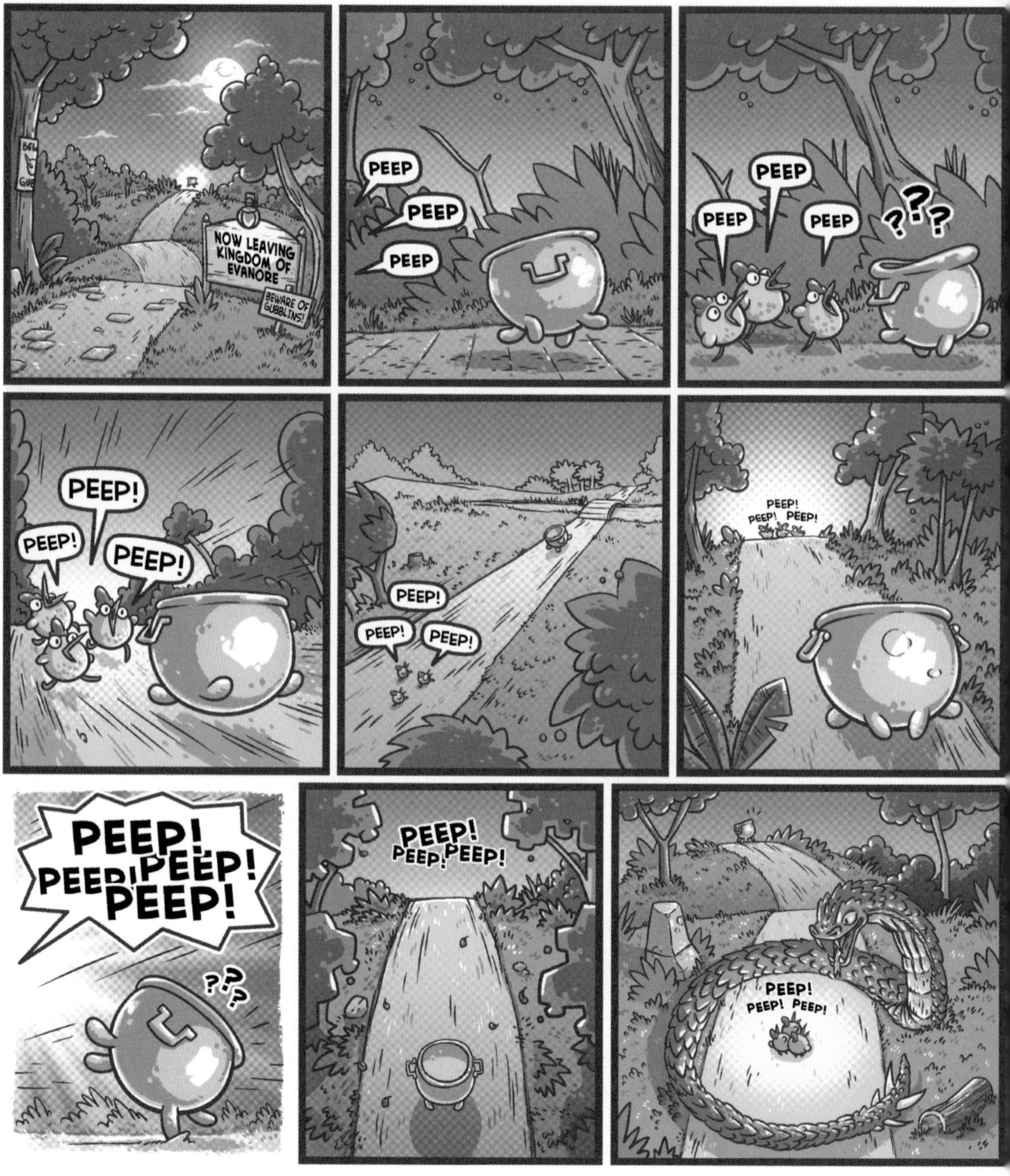
NOW LEAVING KINGDOM OF EVANORE
BEWARE OF GUBBLINS!
PEEP
PEEP
PEEP
PEEP
PEEP
PEEP
???
PEEP!
PEEP!
PEEP!
PEEP!
PEEP!
PEEP!
PEEP!
PEEP! PEEP!
PEEP! PEEP! PEEP! PEEP!
???
PEEP! PEEP! PEEP!
PEEP! PEEP! PEEP!

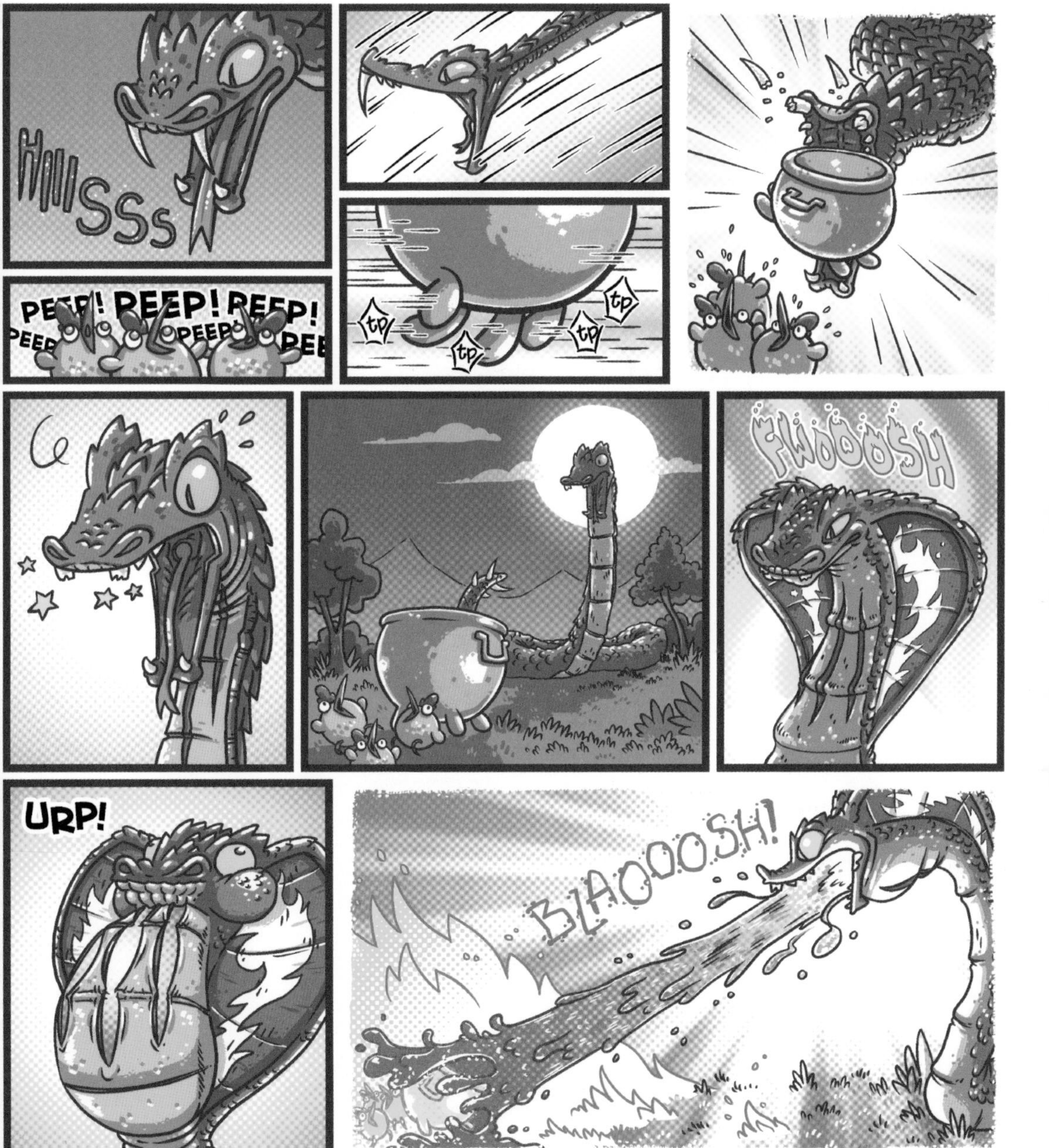
HIIISSS
PEEP! PEEP! PEEP!
tp
tp
tp
tp
FWOOOSH
URP!
BLAOOOSH!

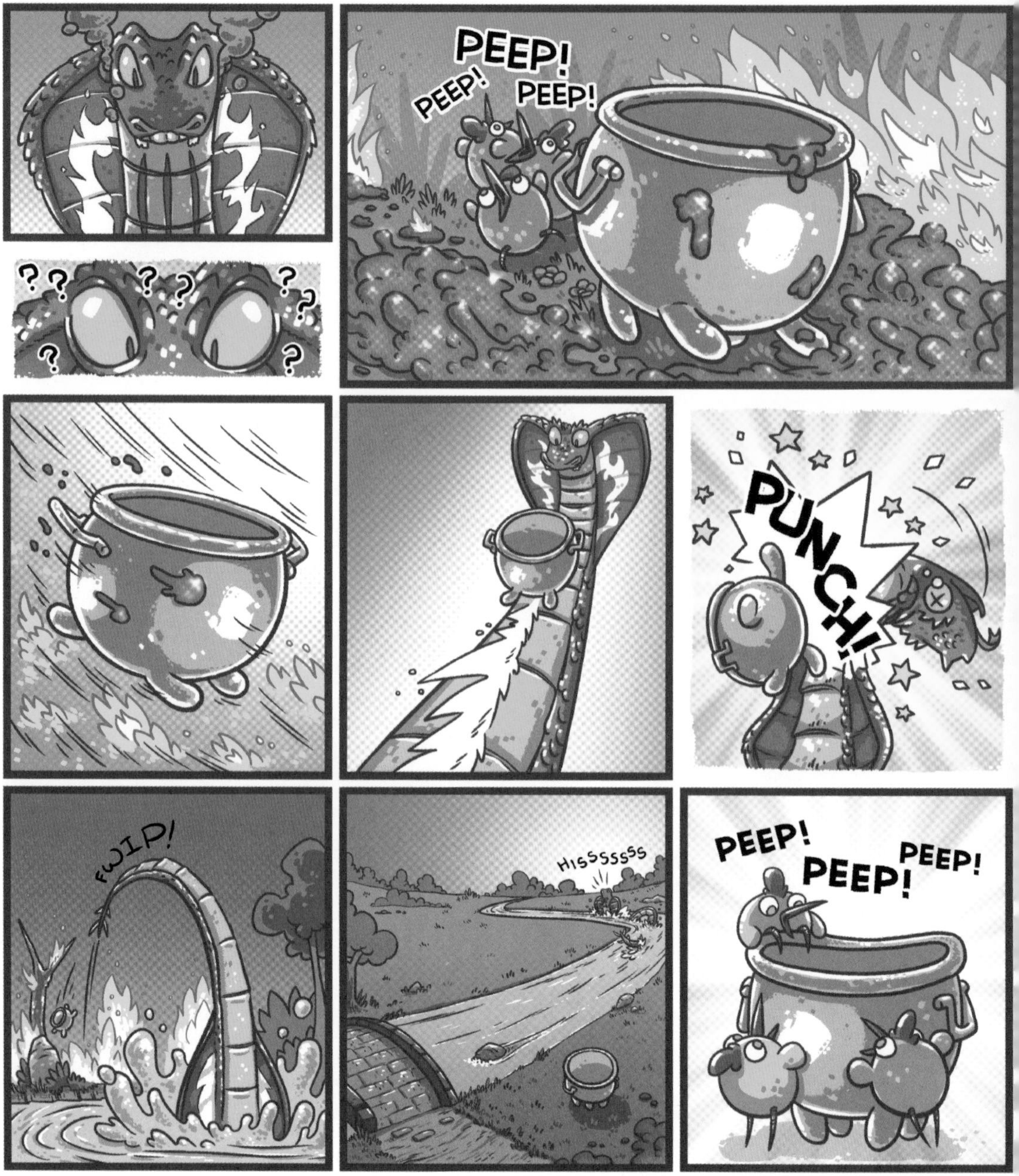
PEEP!
PEEP!
PEEP!
PUNCH!
FWIP!
HISSSSSSS
PEEP!
PEEP!
PEEP!

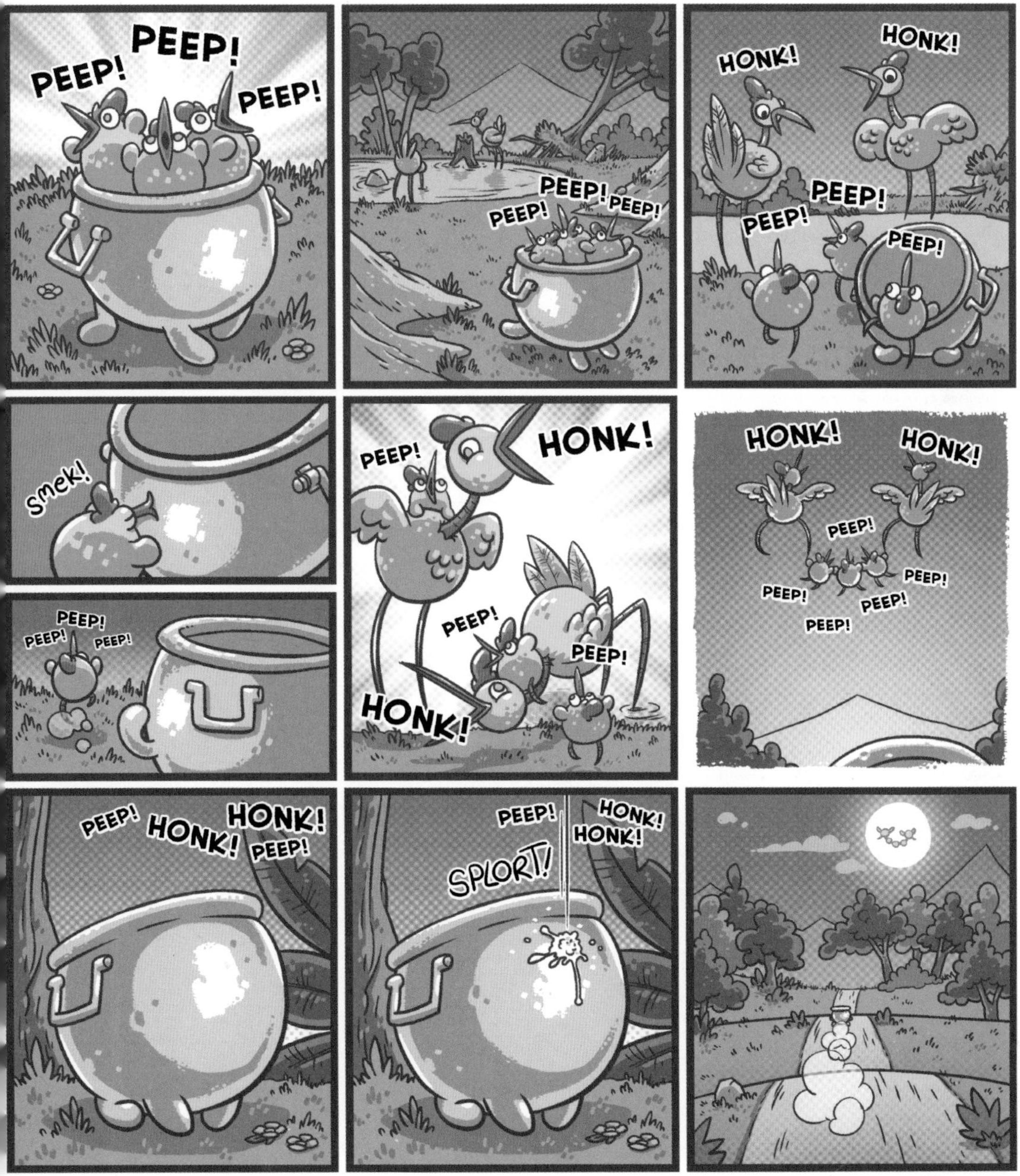
PEEP!
PEEP!
PEEP!
PEEP!
PEEP!
PEEP!
HONK!
HONK!
PEEP!
PEEP!
PEEP!
smek!
PEEP!
PEEP!
PEEP!
PEEP!
HONK!
PEEP!
PEEP!
HONK!
HONK!
HONK!
PEEP!
PEEP!
PEEP!
PEEP!
PEEP!
PEEP!
HONK!
HONK!
PEEP!
PEEP!
HONK!
HONK!
HONK!
SPLORT!

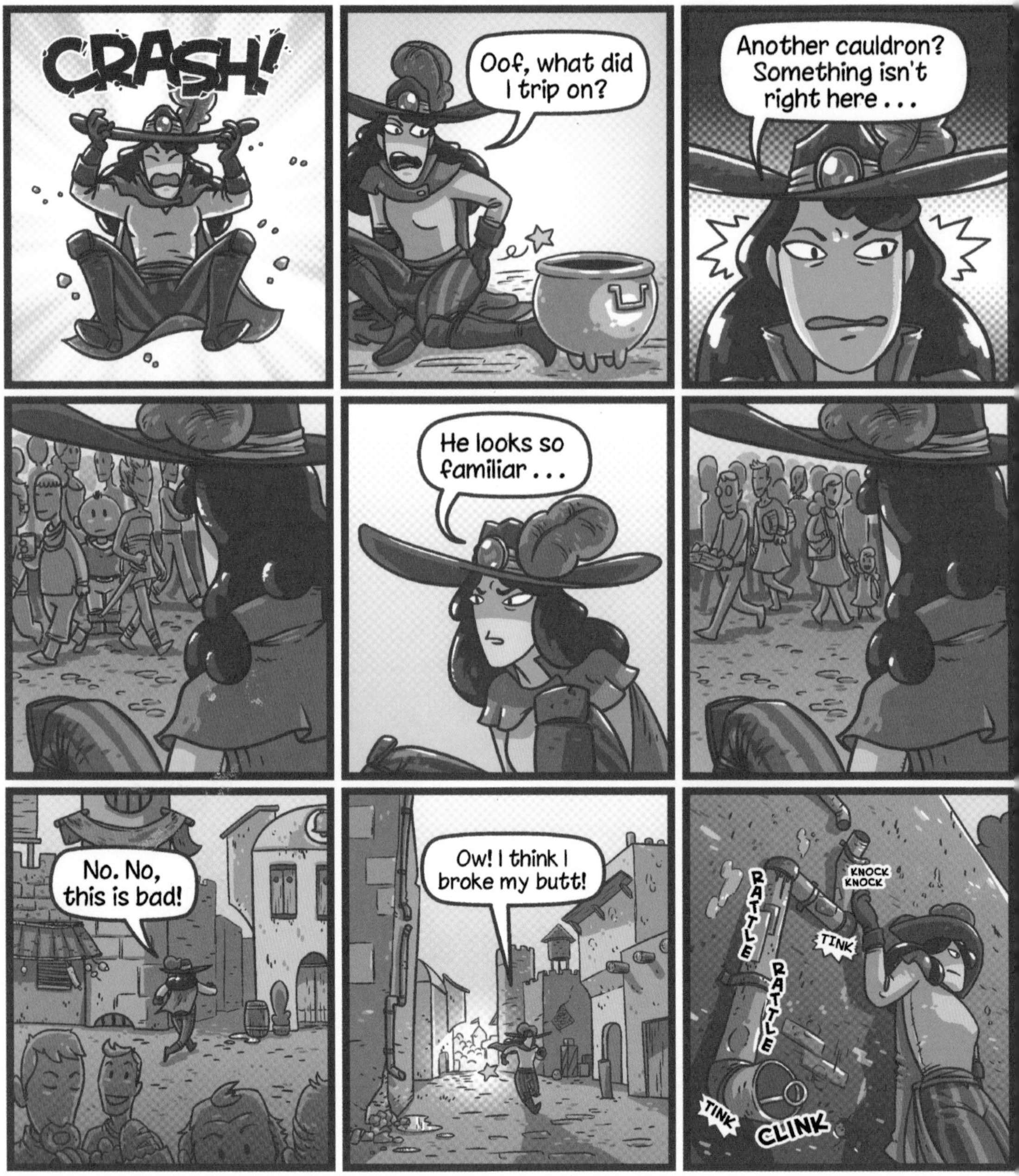
CRASH!
Oof, what did I trip on?
Another cauldron? Something isn't right here . . .
He looks so familiar . . .
No. No, this is bad!
Ow! I think I broke my butt!
KNOCK KNOCK
RATTLE
TINK
RATTLE
TINK
CLINK

69

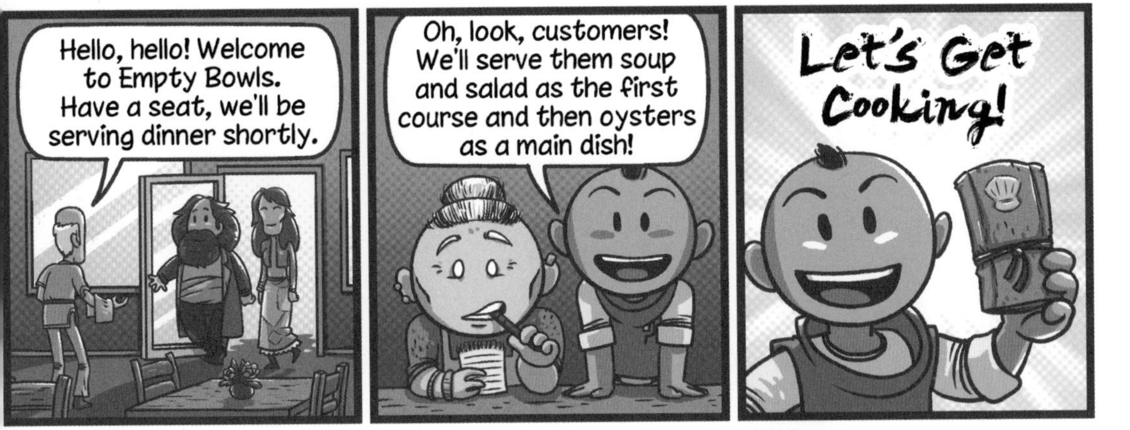
Hello, hello! Welcome to Empty Bowls. Have a seat, we'll be serving dinner shortly.
Oh, look, customers! We'll serve them soup and salad as the first course and then oysters as a main dish!
Let's Get Cooking!

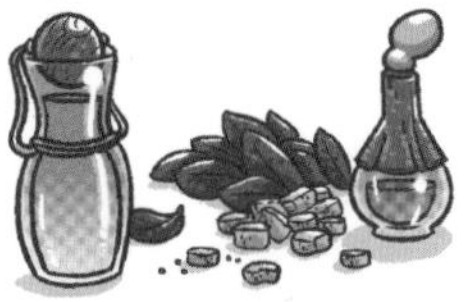

1. Combine oil, spinach, bread crumbs, parsley, salt, and hot sauce.

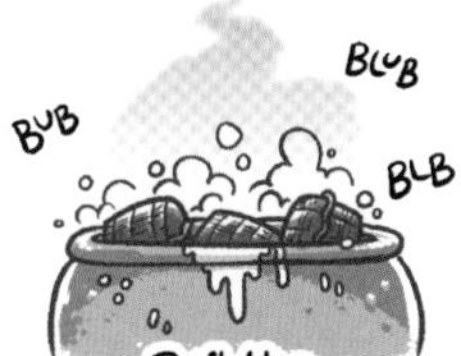
BUB
BLUB
BLB

2. Boil the oysters!

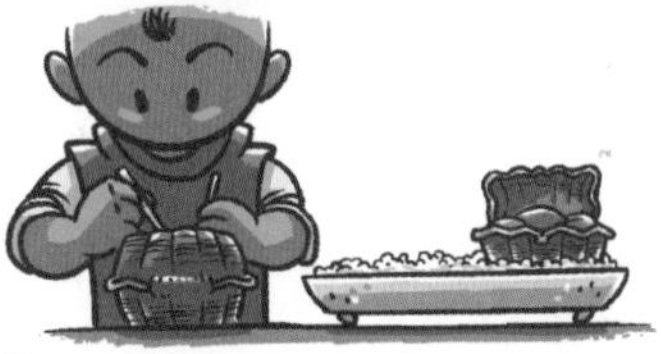

3. Pick the locks and place oysters on a bed of sea salt. Don't spill those juices!

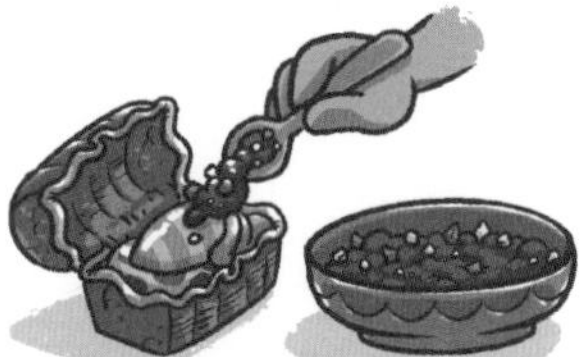

4. Spoon spinach mixture onto the oysters and bake for 10 minutes.

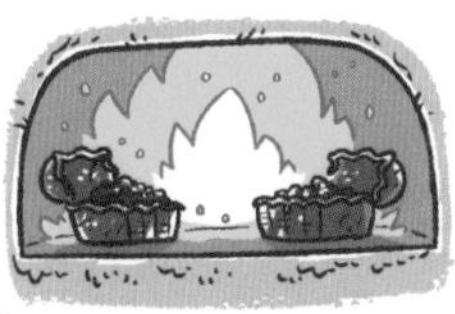

5. Add cheese and bacon. Broil until it's all melty!

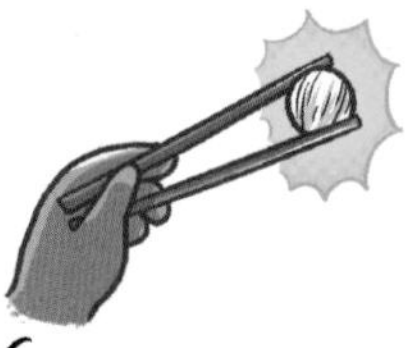

6. Finally, add a single pickled pearl onion to the top and serve!

You have made

A SUNKEN TREASURE OYSTER!

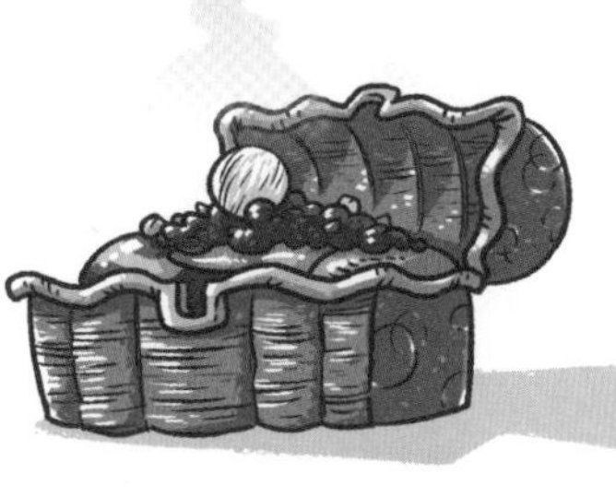

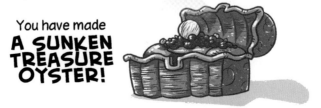

74

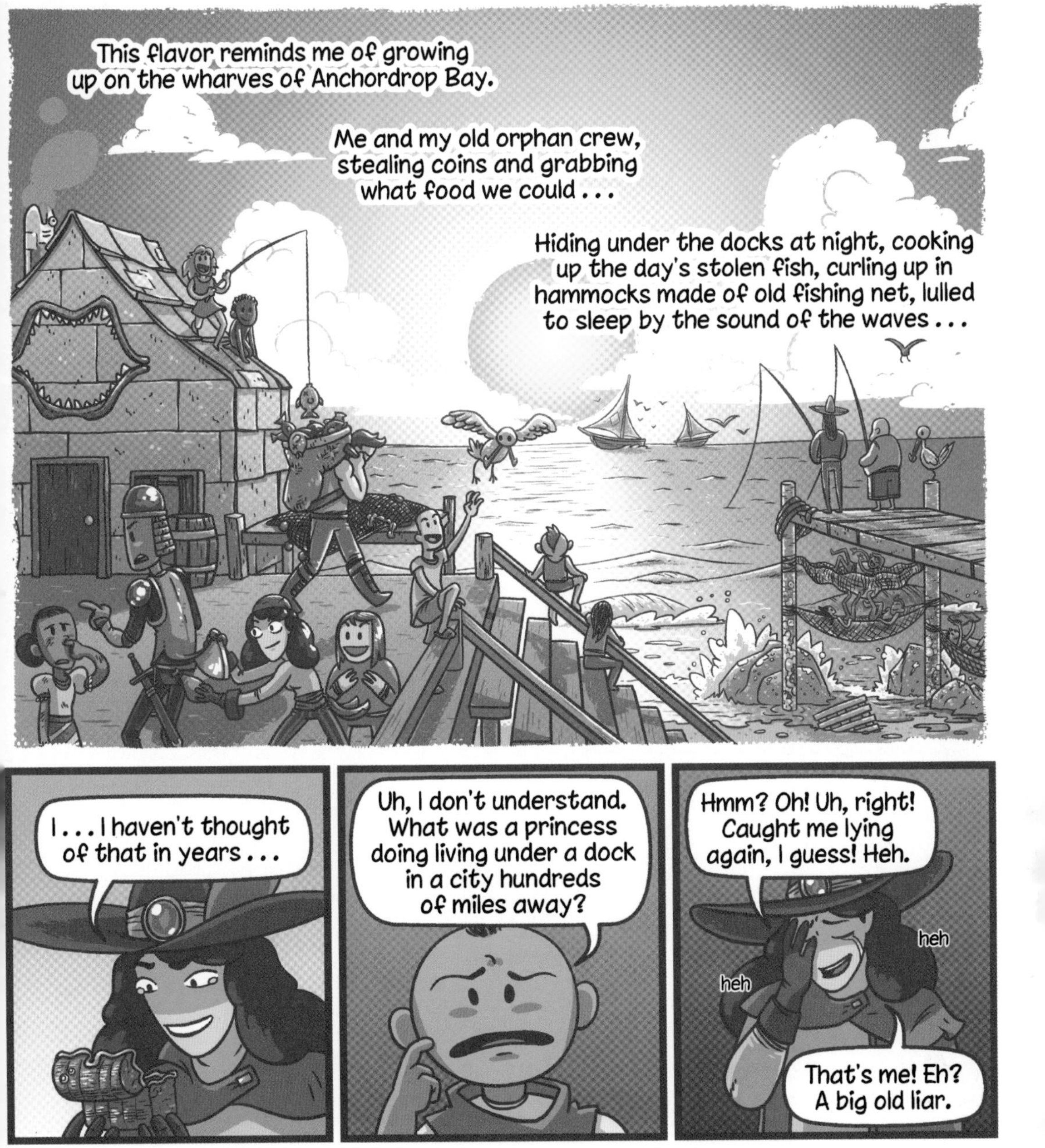
This flavor reminds me of growing up on the wharves of Anchordrop Bay.
Me and my old orphan crew, stealing coins and grabbing what food we could . . .
Hiding under the docks at night, cooking up the day's stolen fish, curling up in hammocks made of old fishing net, lulled to sleep by the sound of the waves . . .
I . . . I haven't thought of that in years . . .
Uh, I don't understand. What was a princess doing living under a dock in a city hundreds of miles away?
Hmm? Oh! Uh, right! Caught me lying again, I guess! Heh.
heh
heh
That's me! Eh? A big old liar.

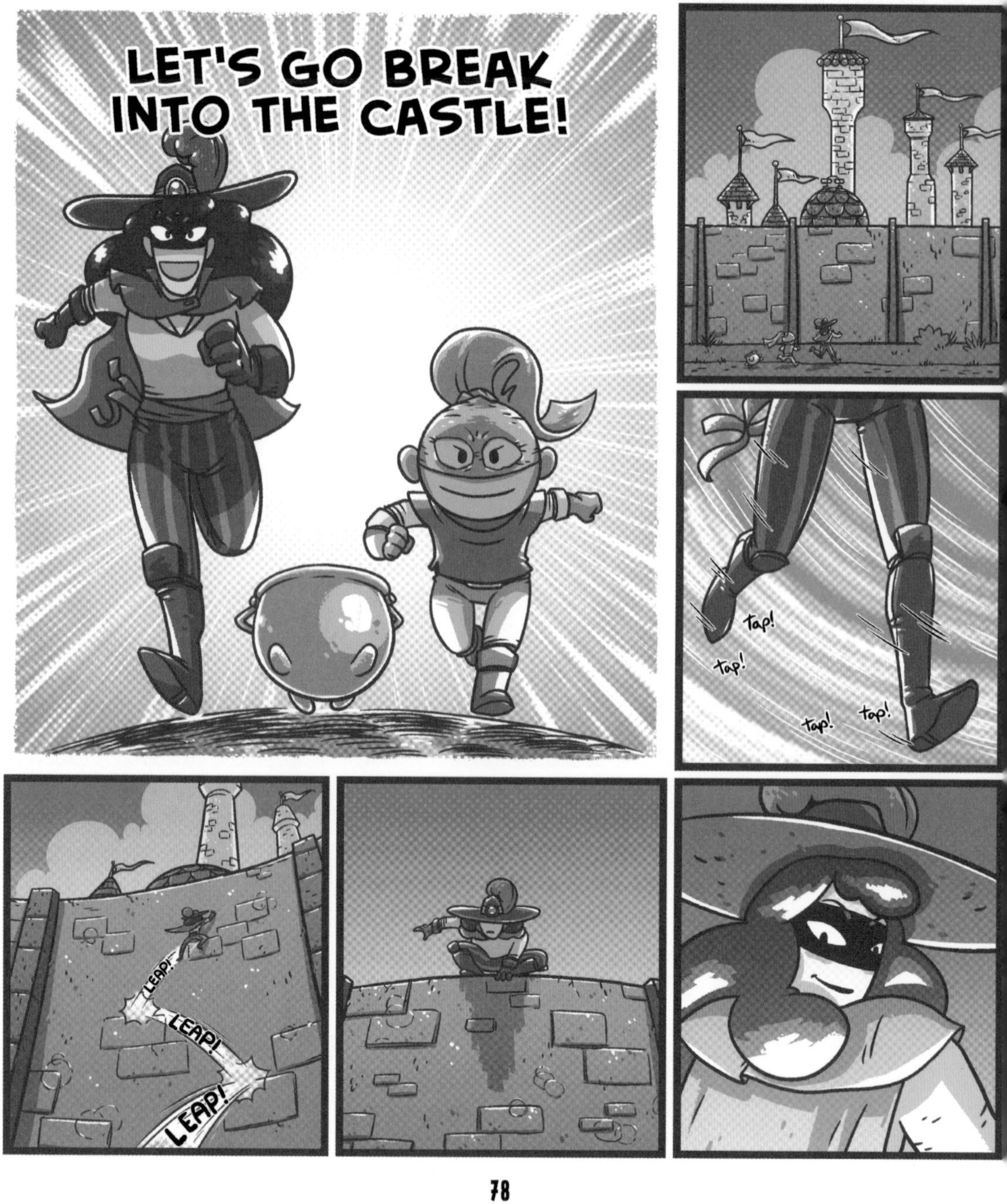
LET'S GO BREAK INTO THE CASTLE!
Tap!
tap!
tap!
tap!
LEAP!
LEAP!
LEAP!
LEAP!

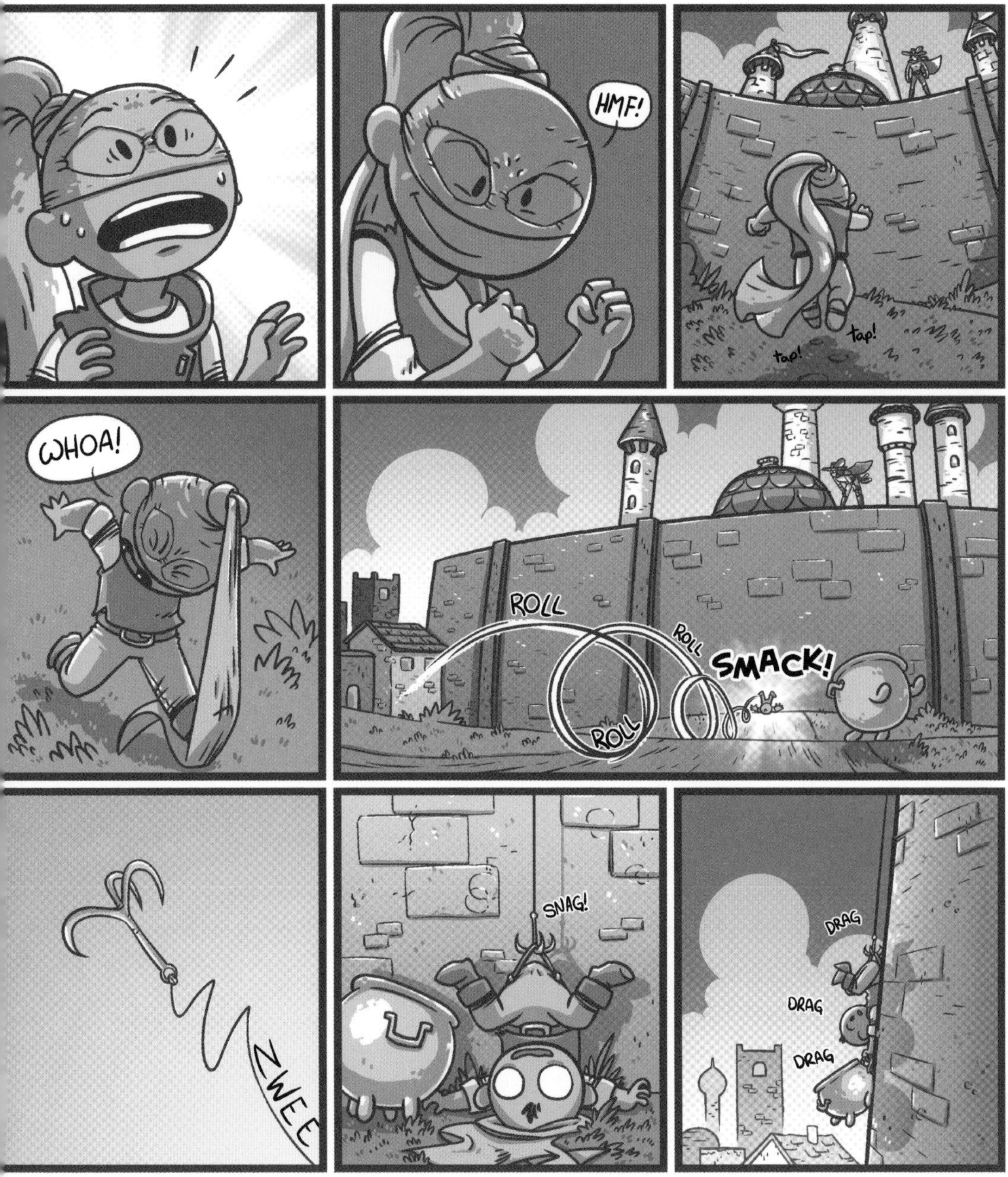
HMF!
tap!
tap!
WHOA!
ROLL
ROLL
ROLL
SMACK!
ZWEE
SNAG!
DRAG
DRAG
DRAG

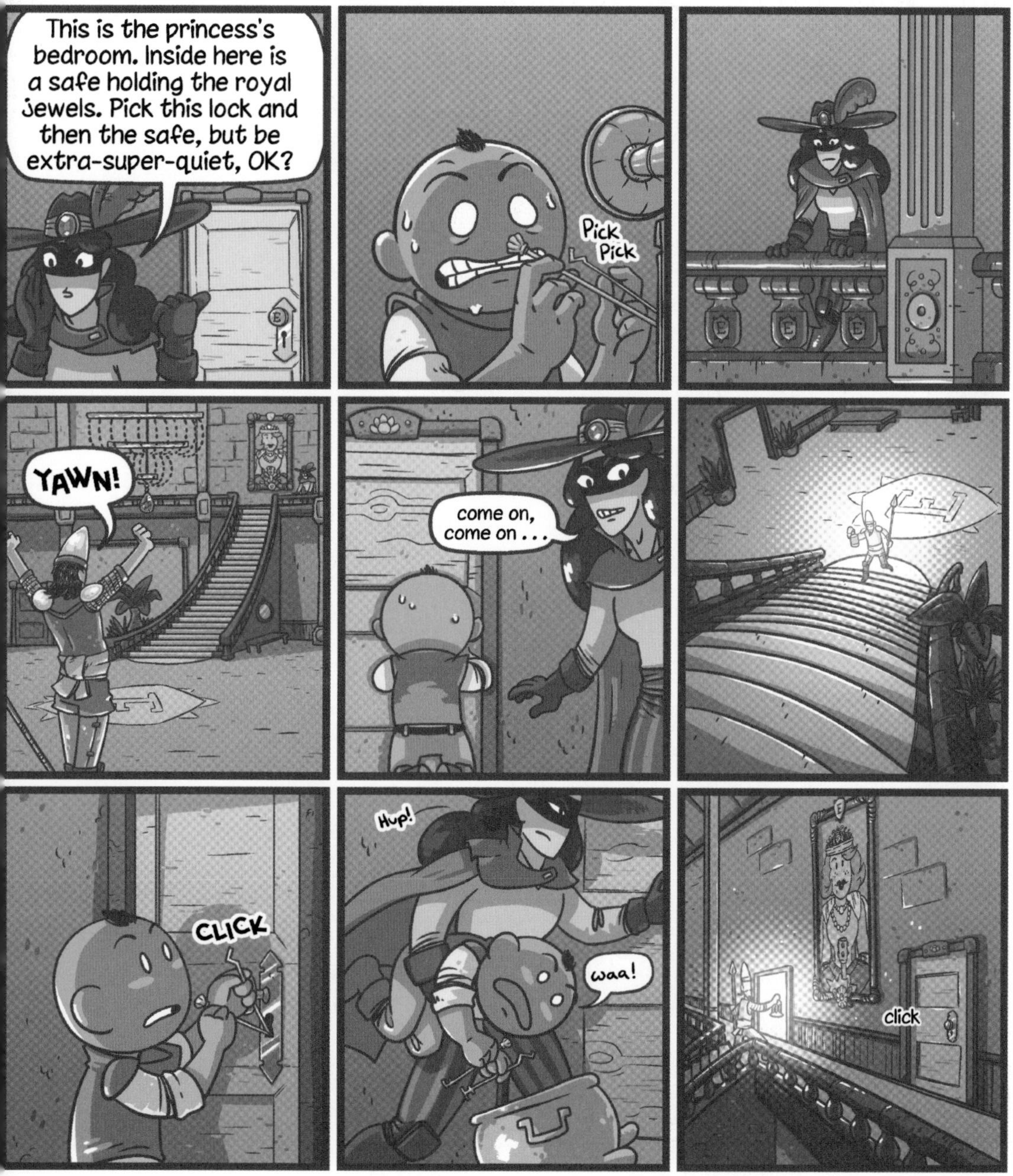

This is the princess's bedroom. Inside here is a safe holding the royal jewels. Pick this lock and then the safe, but be extra-super-quiet, OK?
Pick
Pick
YAWN!
come on, come on . . .
CLICK
Hup!
waa!
click

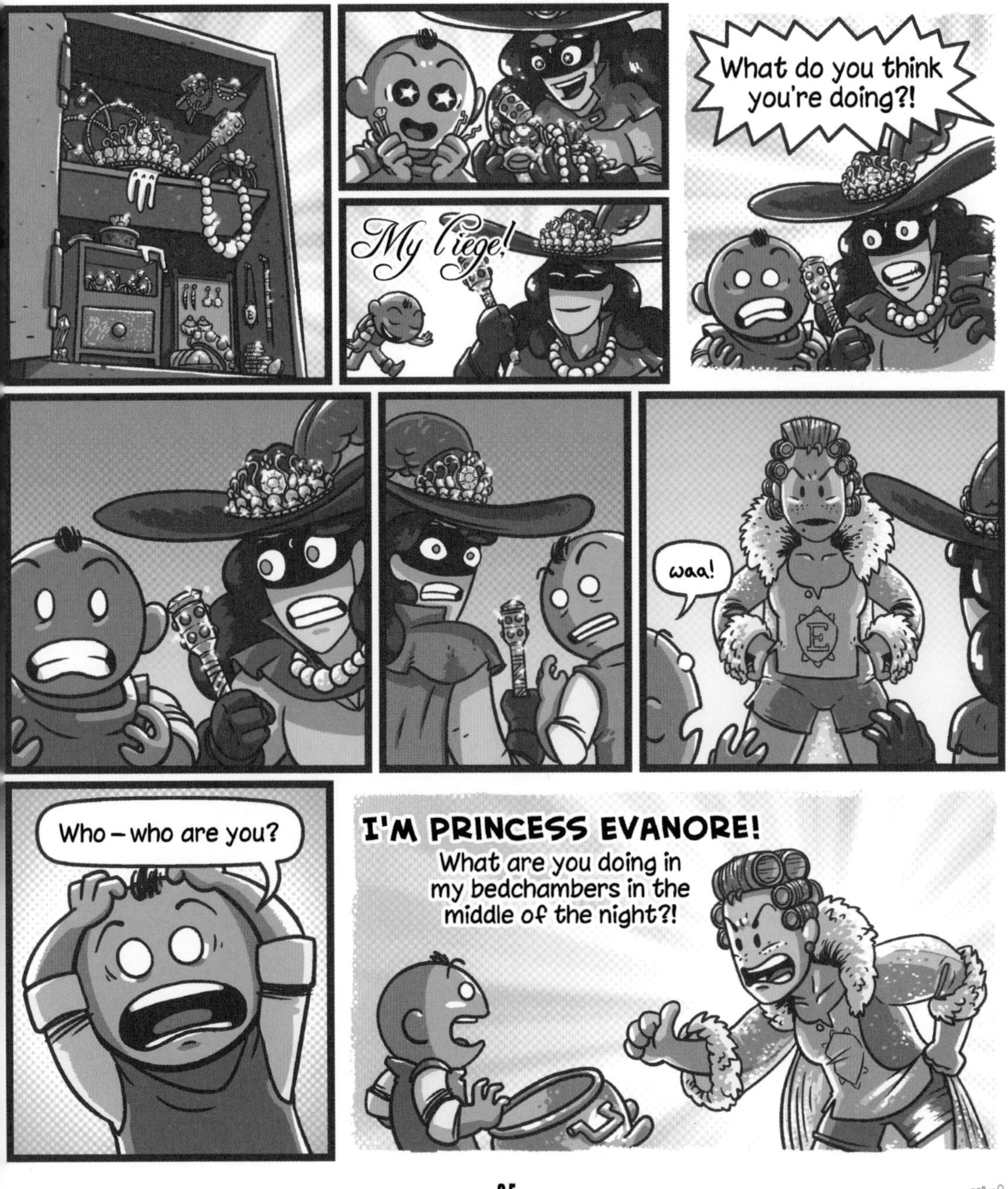
My liege!
What do you think you're doing?!
waa!
Who—who are you?
I'M PRINCESS EVANORE!
What are you doing in my bedchambers in the middle of the night?!

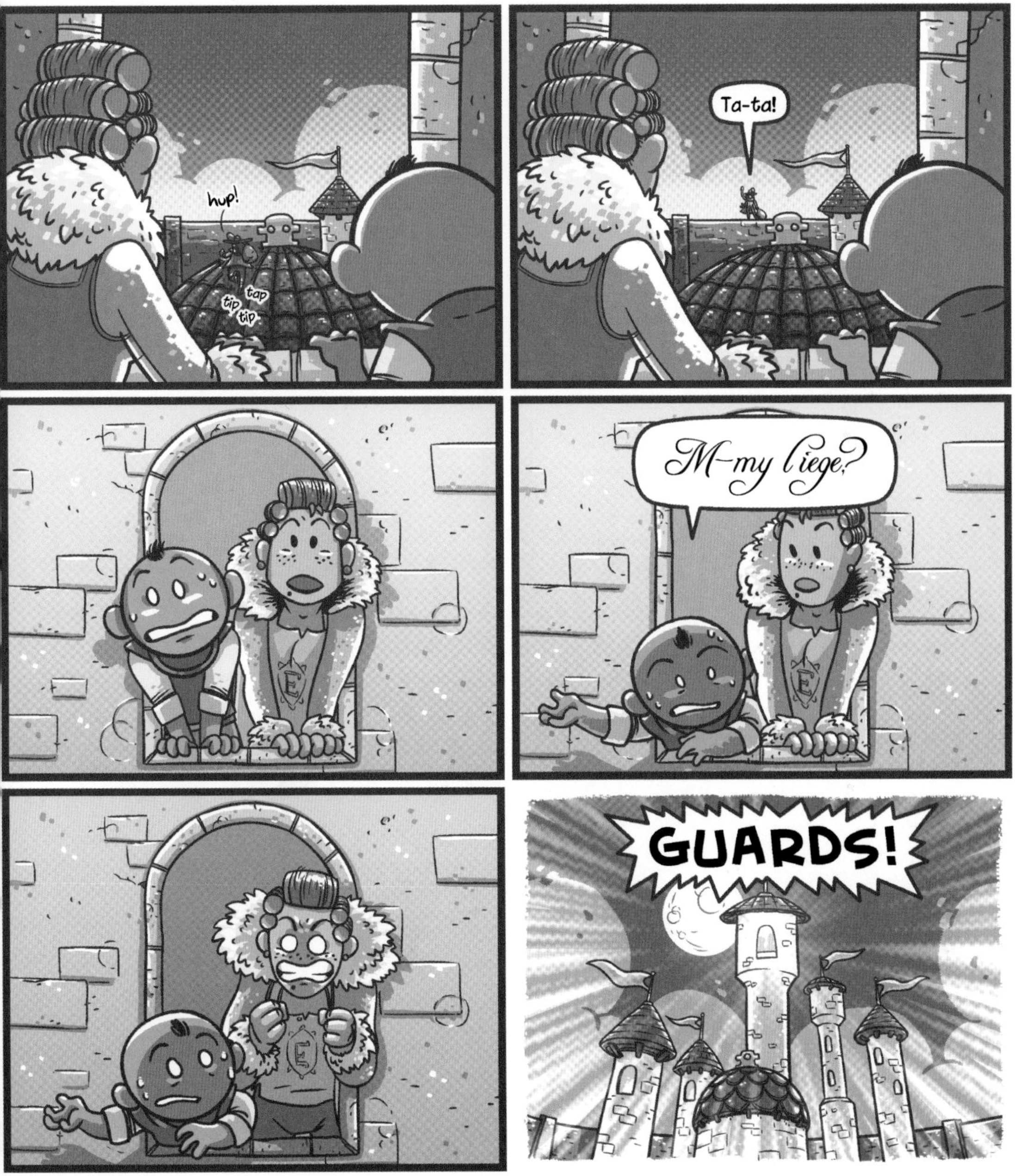
hup!
tip
tap
tip
Ta-ta!
M-my liege?
GUARDS!

End of
Chapter Three

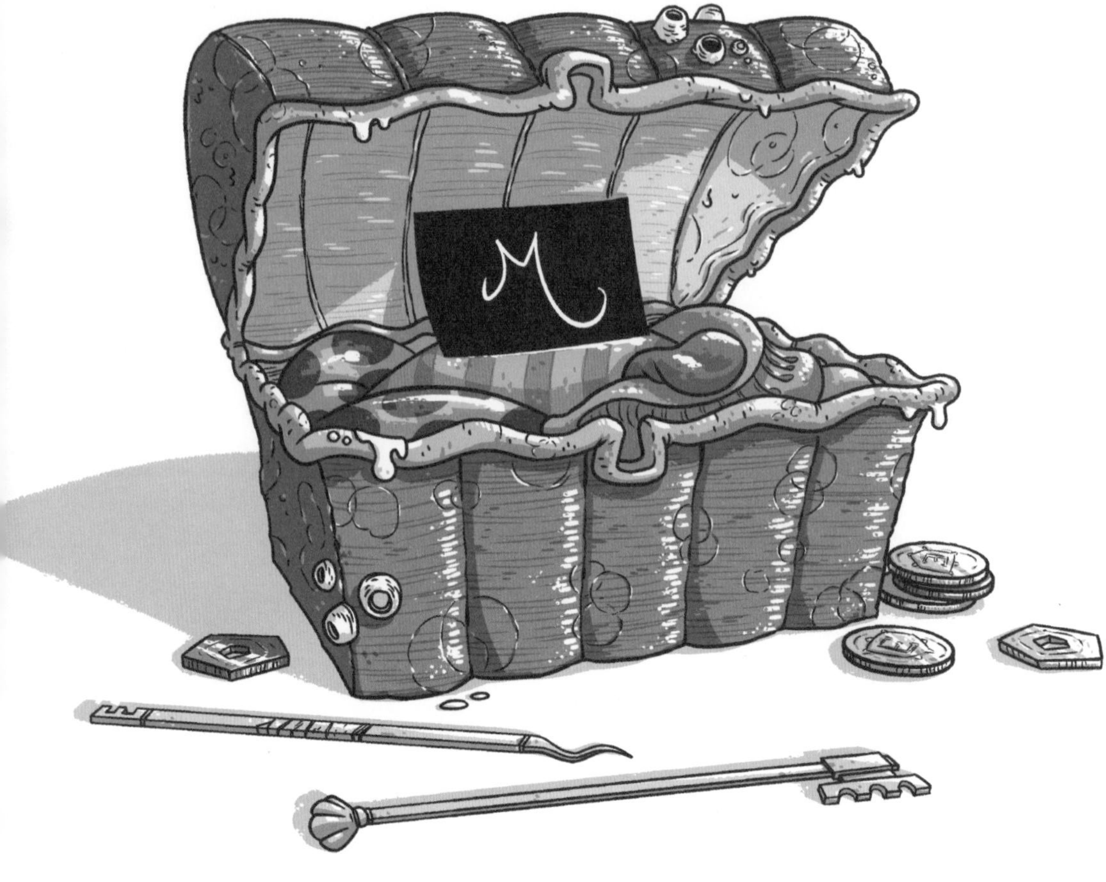

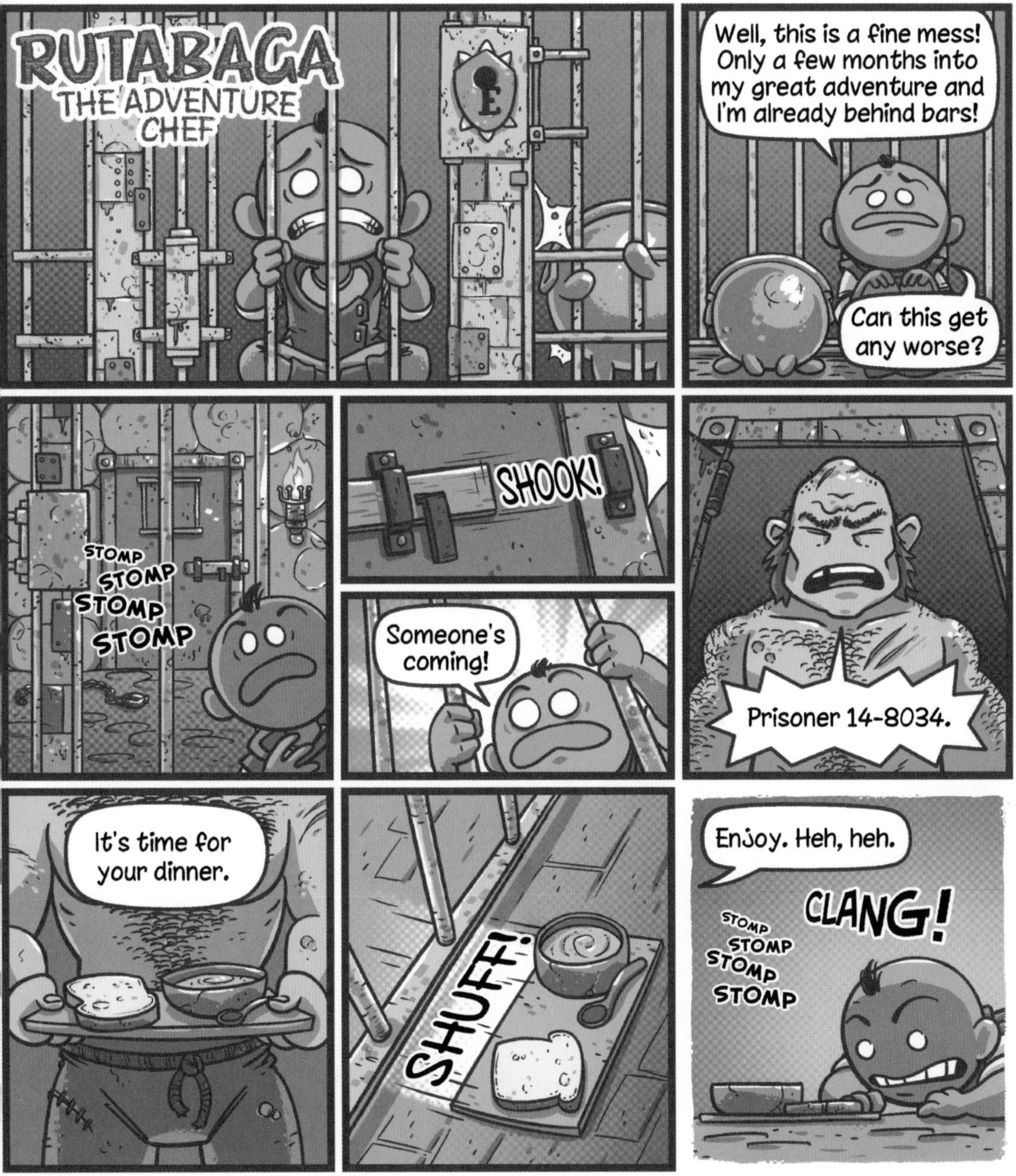

RUTABAGA
THE ADVENTURE CHEF
Well, this is a fine mess! Only a few months into my great adventure and I'm already behind bars!
Can this get any worse?
STOMP STOMP STOMP STOMP
SHOOK!
Someone's coming!
Prisoner 14-8034.
It's time for your dinner.
SHUFF!
Enjoy. Heh, heh.
CLANG!
STOMP STOMP STOMP STOMP

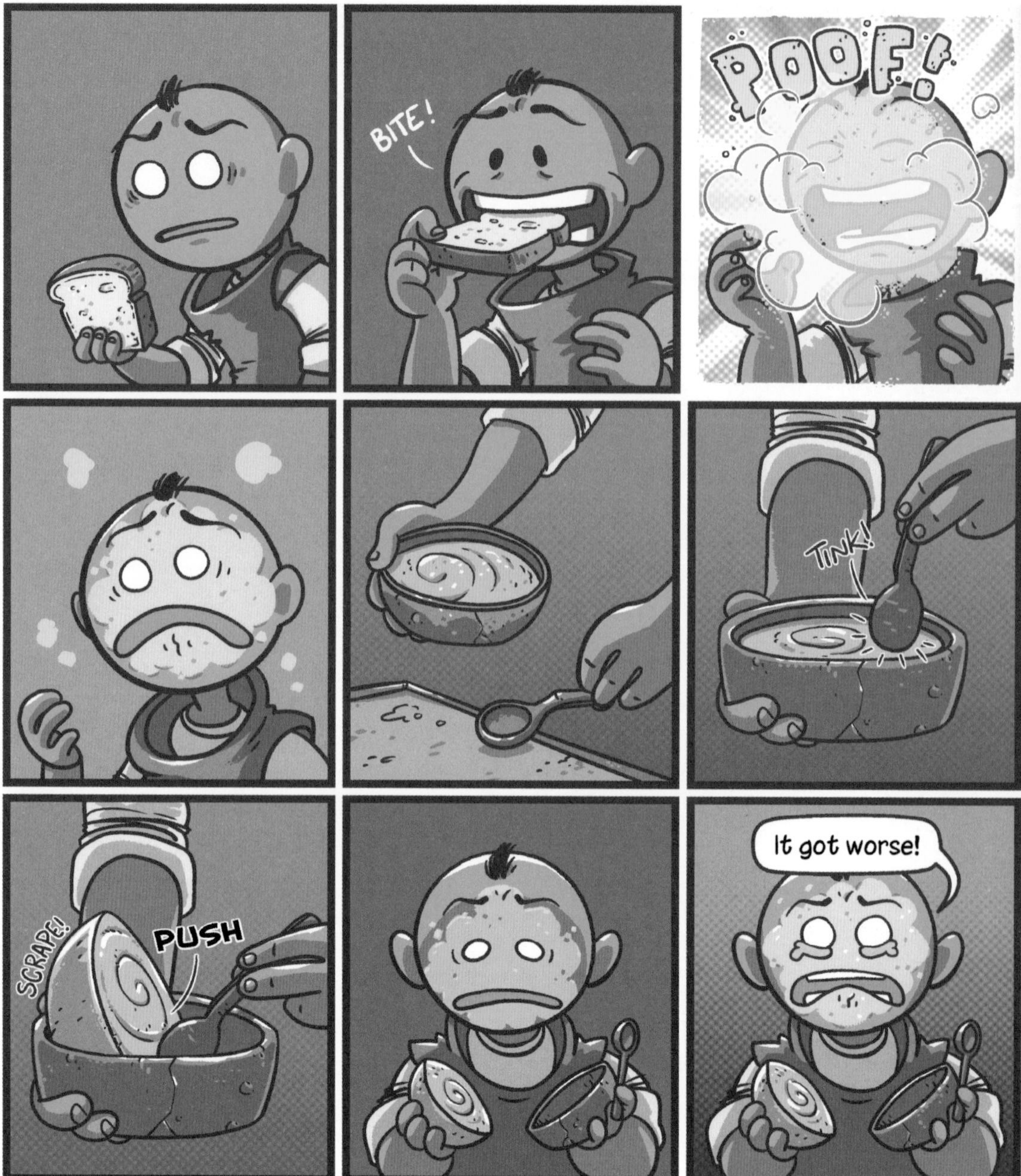
BITE!
POOF!
TINK!
SCRAPE!
PUSH
It got worse!

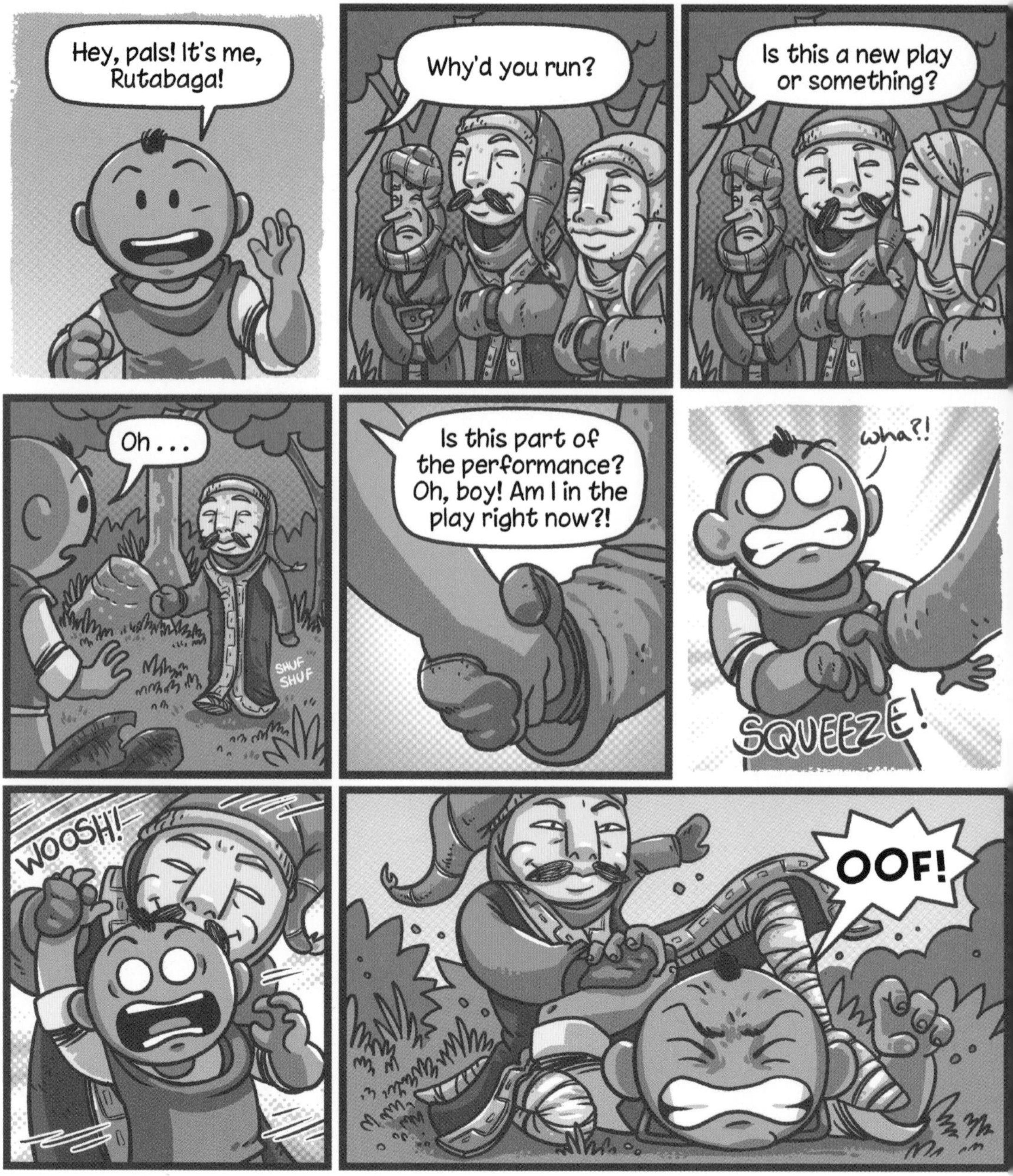
Hey, pals! It's me, Rutabaga!
Why'd you run?
Is this a new play or something?
Oh . . . .
SHUF SHUF
Is this part of the performance? Oh, boy! Am I in the play right now?!
wha?!
SQUEEZE!
WOOSH!
OOF!

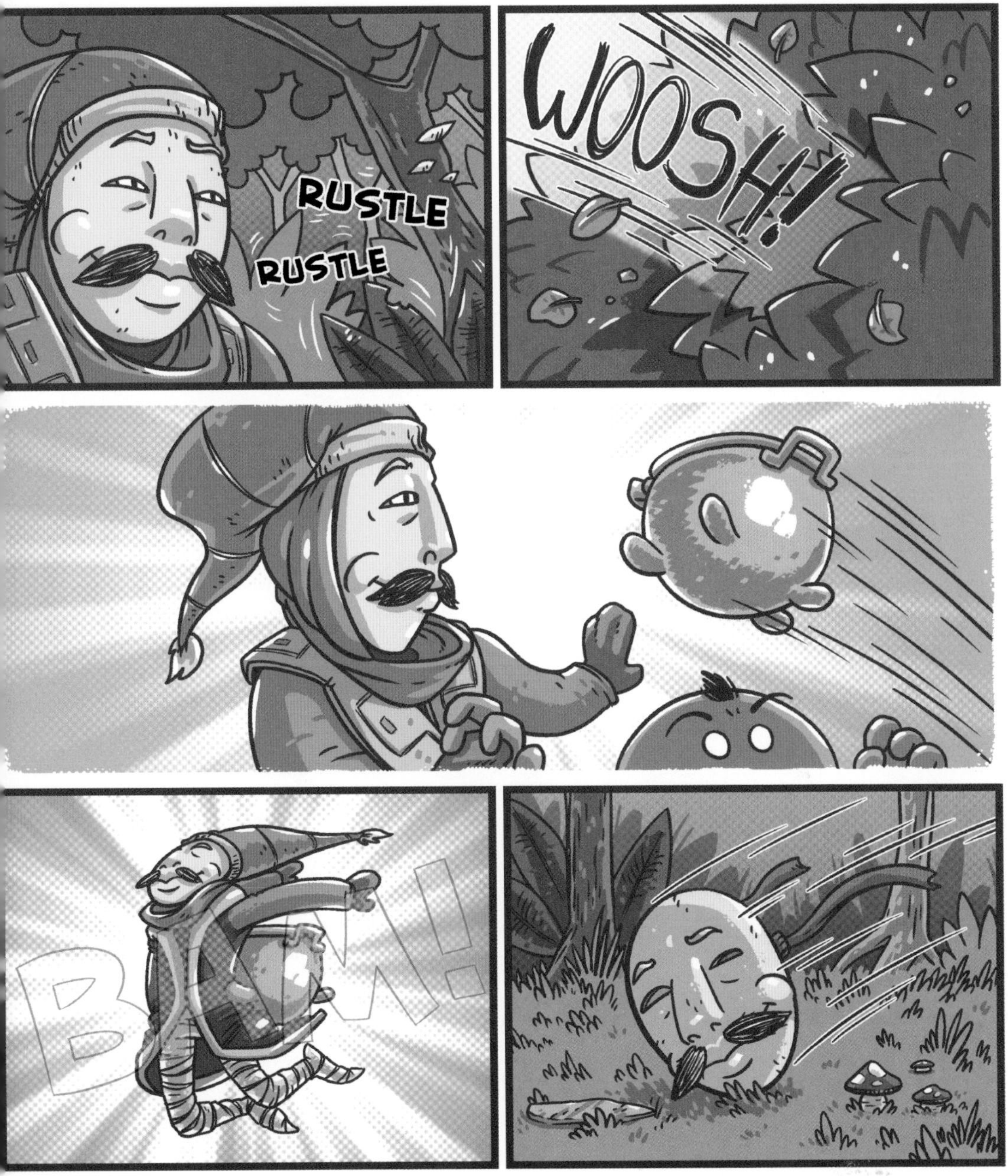
RUSTLE
RUSTLE
WOOSH!
BAM!

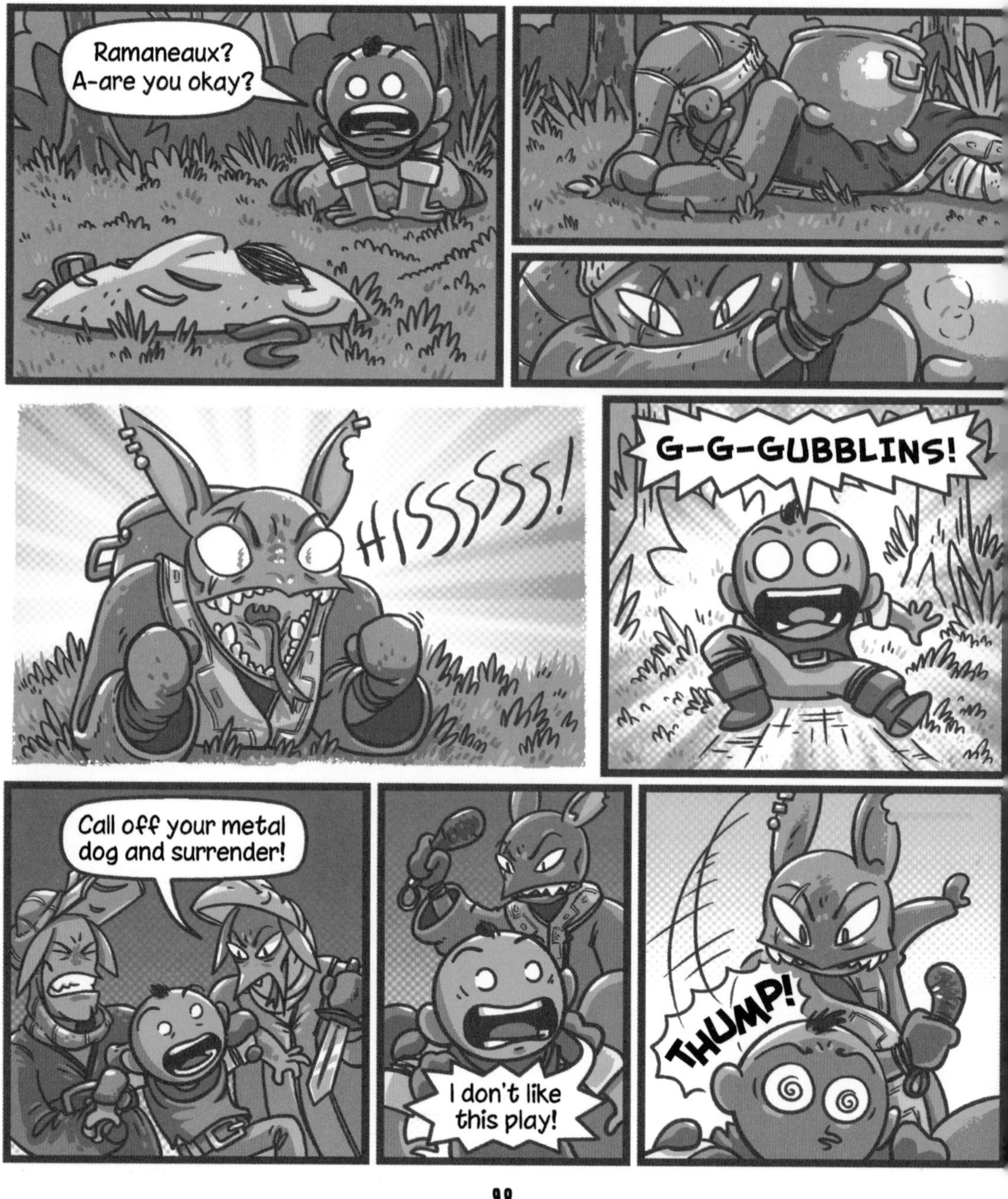
Ramaneaux? A-are you okay?
HISSSSSS!
G-G-GUBBLINS!
Call off your metal dog and surrender!
I don't like this play!
THUMP!

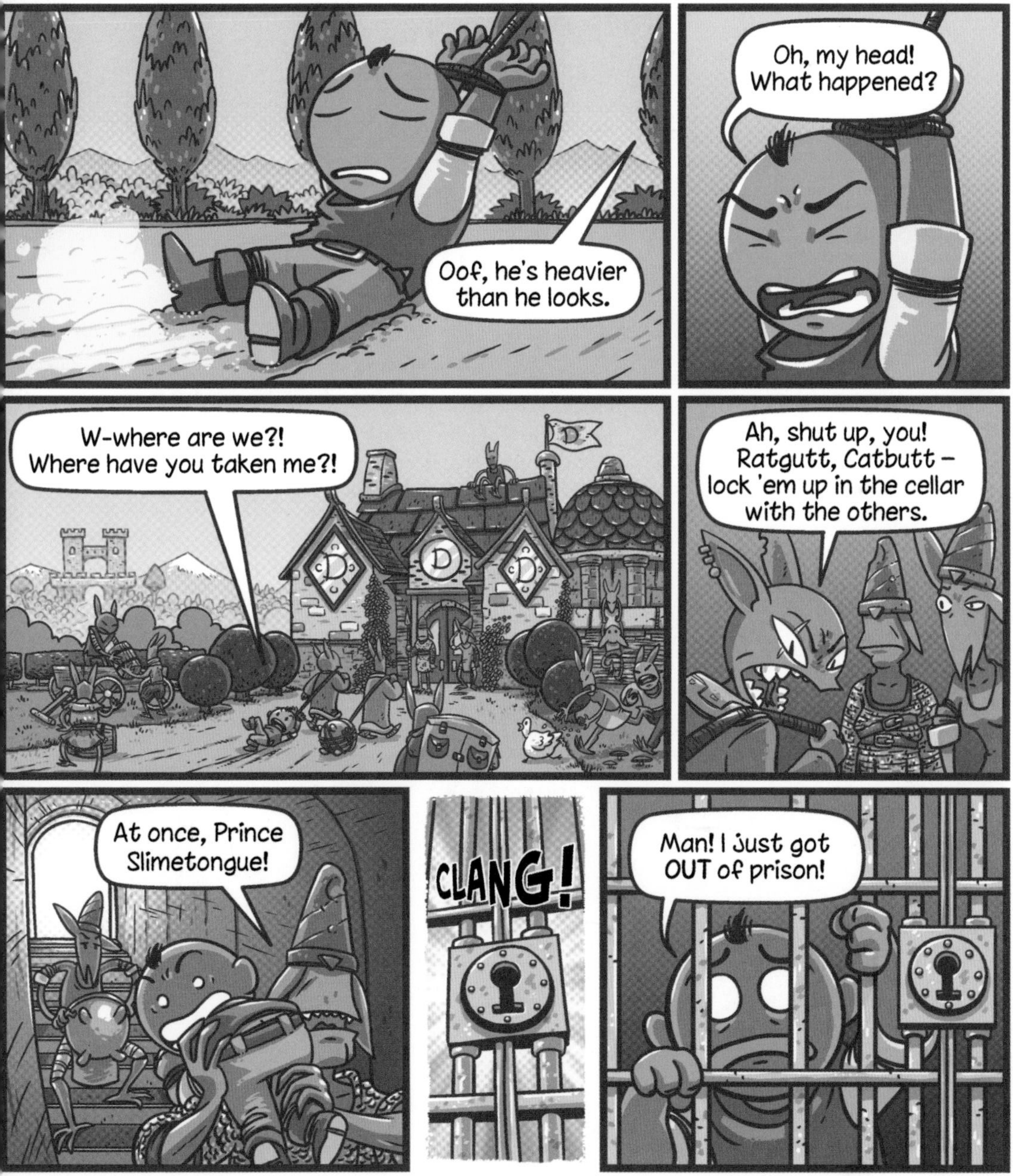
Oof, he's heavier than he looks.
Oh, my head! What happened?
W-where are we?! Where have you taken me?!
Ah, shut up, you! Ratgutt, Catbutt – lock 'em up in the cellar with the others.
At once, Prince Slimetongue!
CLANG!
Man! I just got OUT of prison!

104

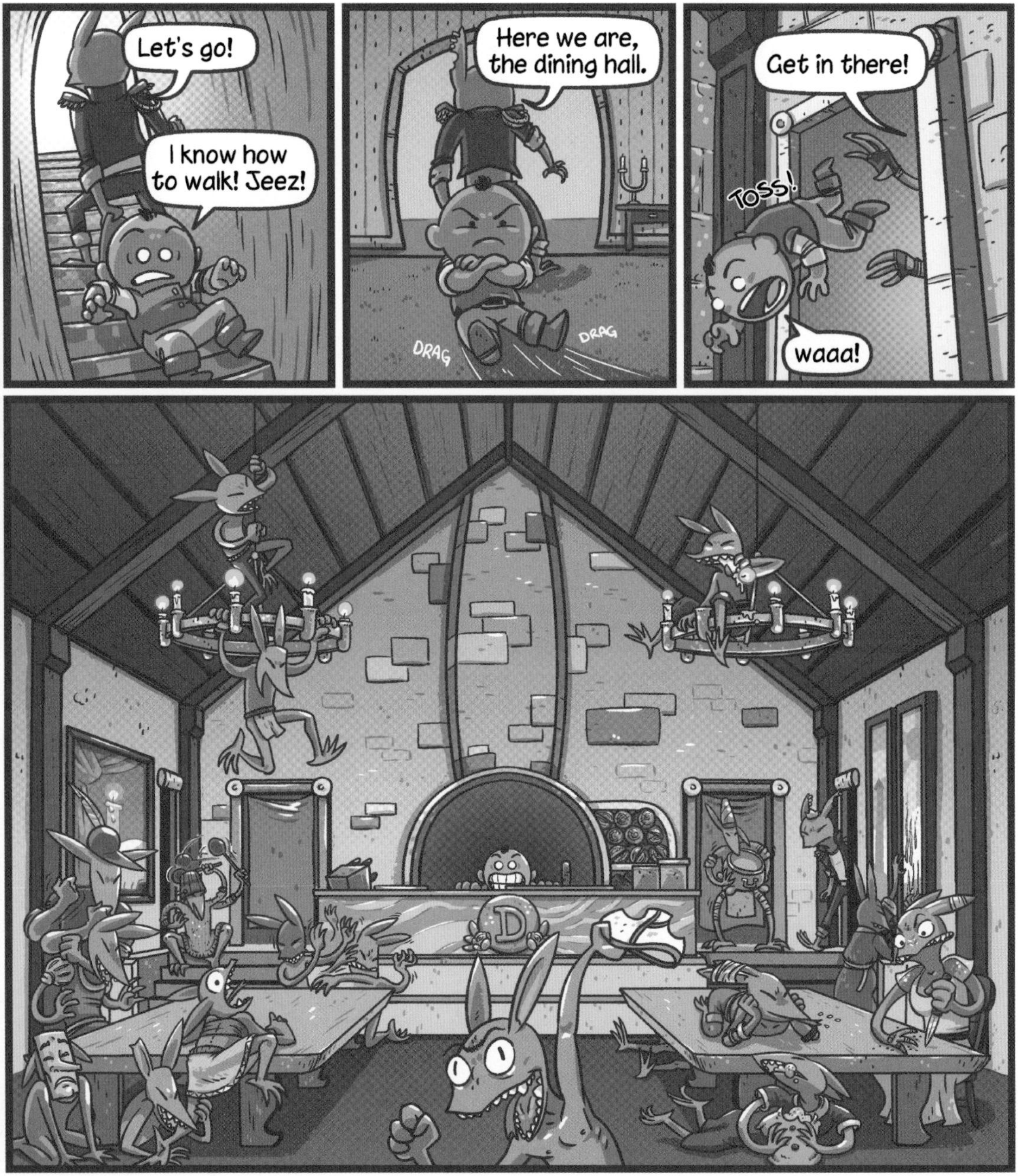
Let's go!
I know how to walk! Jeez!
Here we are, the dining hall.
DRAG
DRAG
Get in there!
TOSS!
waaa!

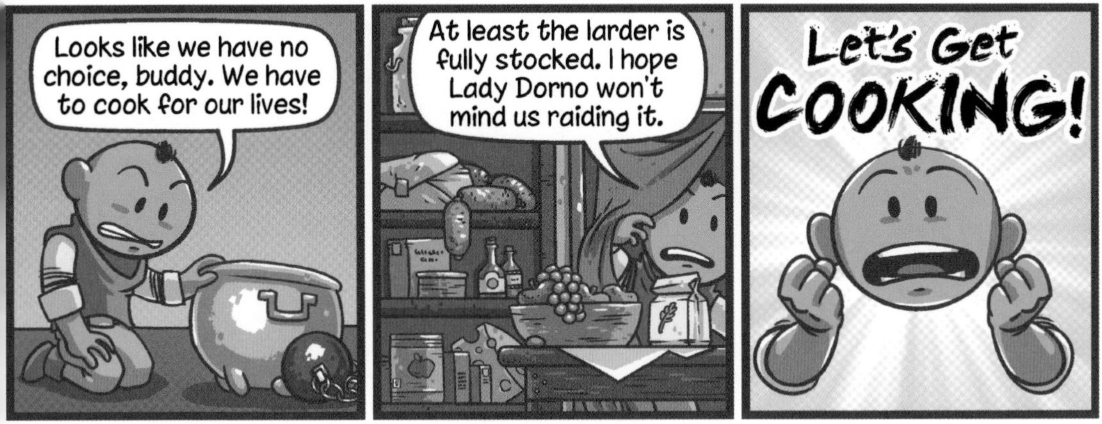
Looks like we have no choice, buddy. We have to cook for our lives!
At least the larder is fully stocked. I hope Lady Dorno won't mind us raiding it.
Let's Get COOKING!

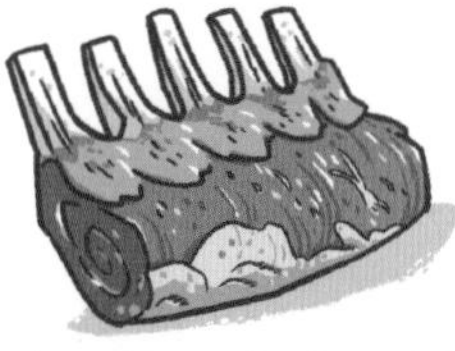

1. Get a nice cut of pork loin with the ribs still intact.

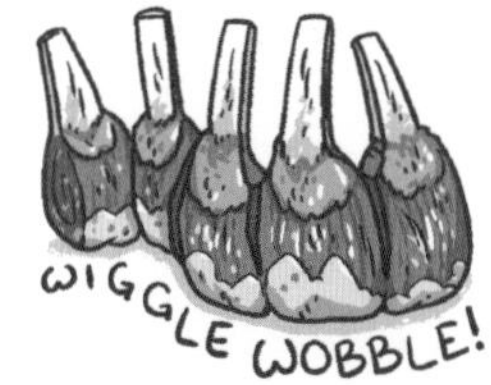
WIGGLE WOBBLE!

2. Cut between the ribs to allow the meat to bend.

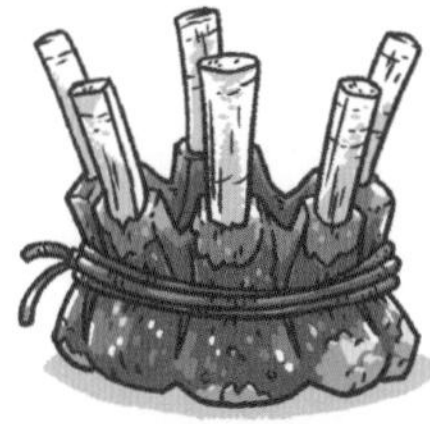

3. Shape the pork loin into a ring and tie it together.

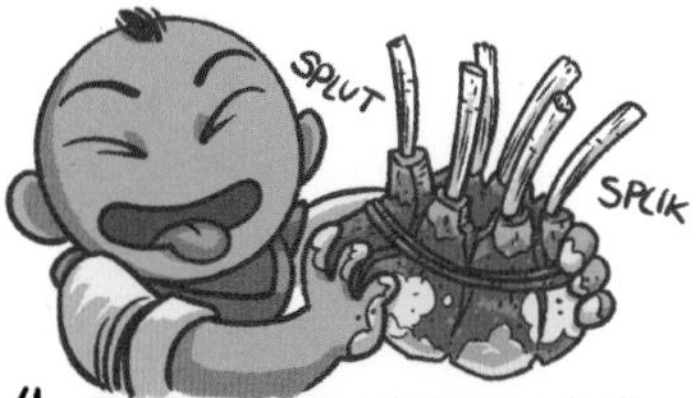
SPLUT
SPLIK

4. Slather on a mixture of oil, salt, pepper, garlic, and spices. Get real messy!

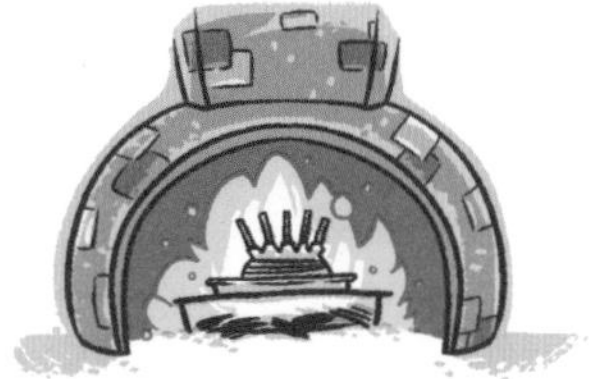

5. Cook in a roasting pan with a bunch of cherries and peeled pears.

You've made a . . .

KING'S CROWN with FRUIT JEWELS

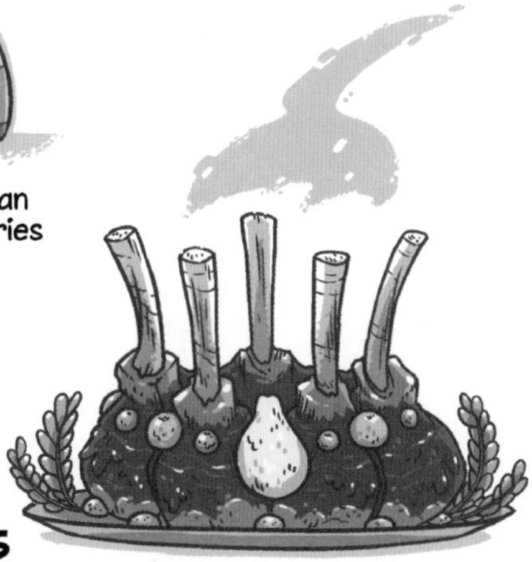

110

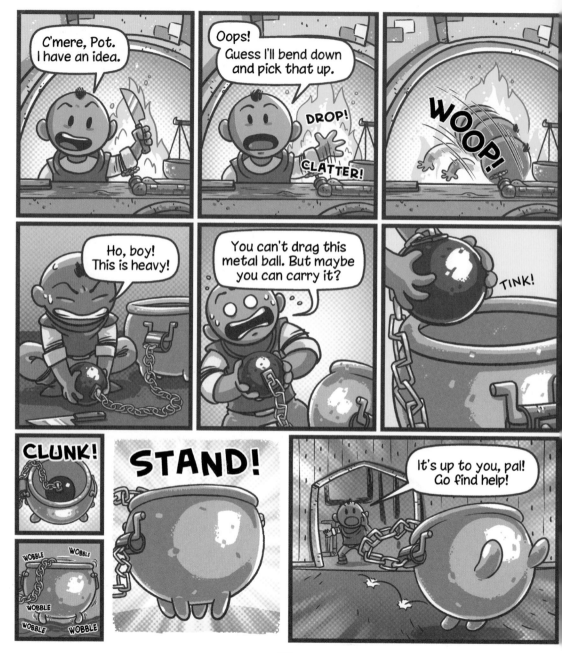

114

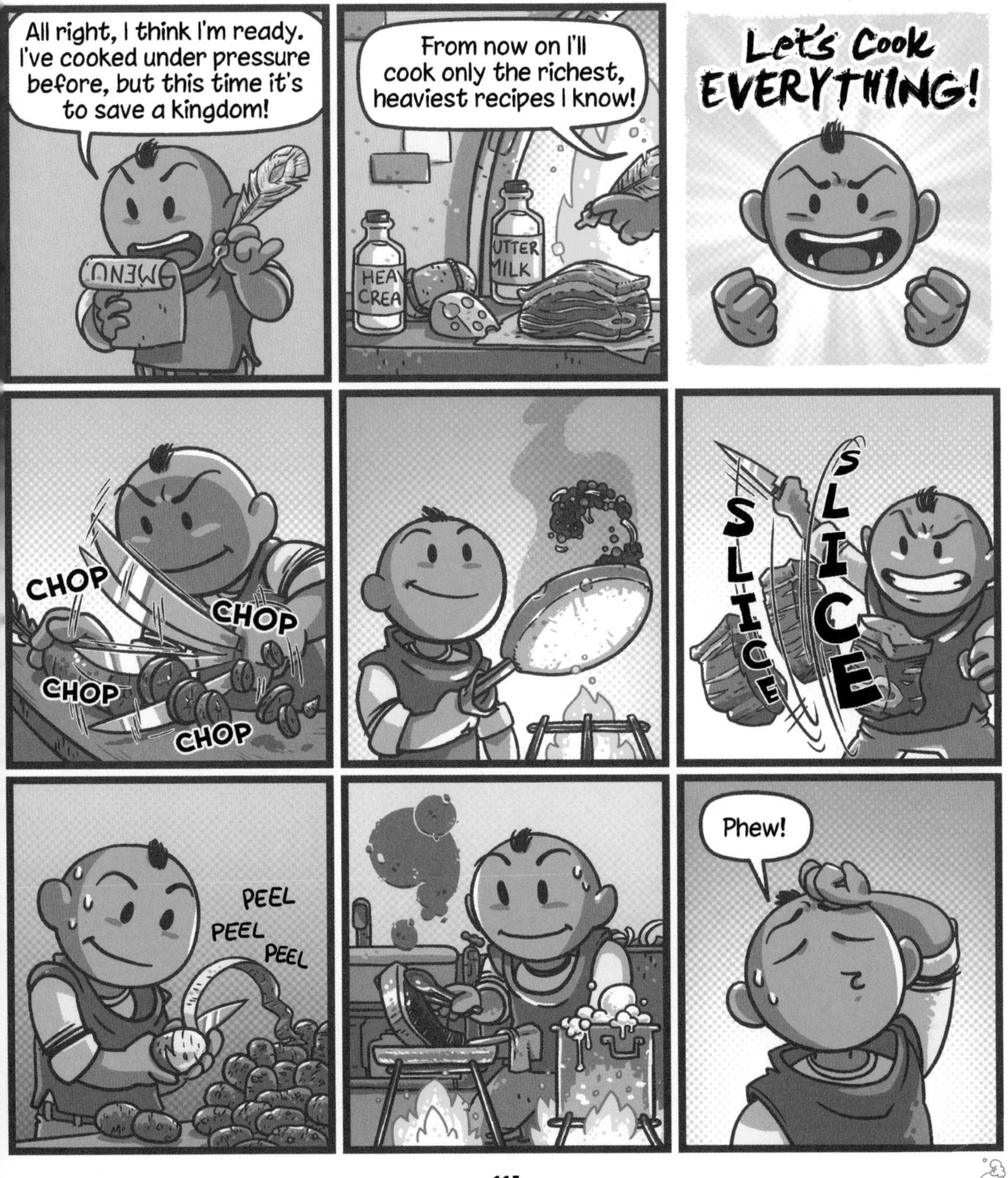
All right, I think I'm ready. I've cooked under pressure before, but this time it's to save a kingdom!
MENU
From now on I'll cook only the richest, heaviest recipes I know!
HEA CREA
UTTER MILK
Let's Cook EVERYTHING!
CHOP
CHOP
CHOP
CHOP
SLICE
SLICE
PEEL
PEEL
PEEL
Phew!

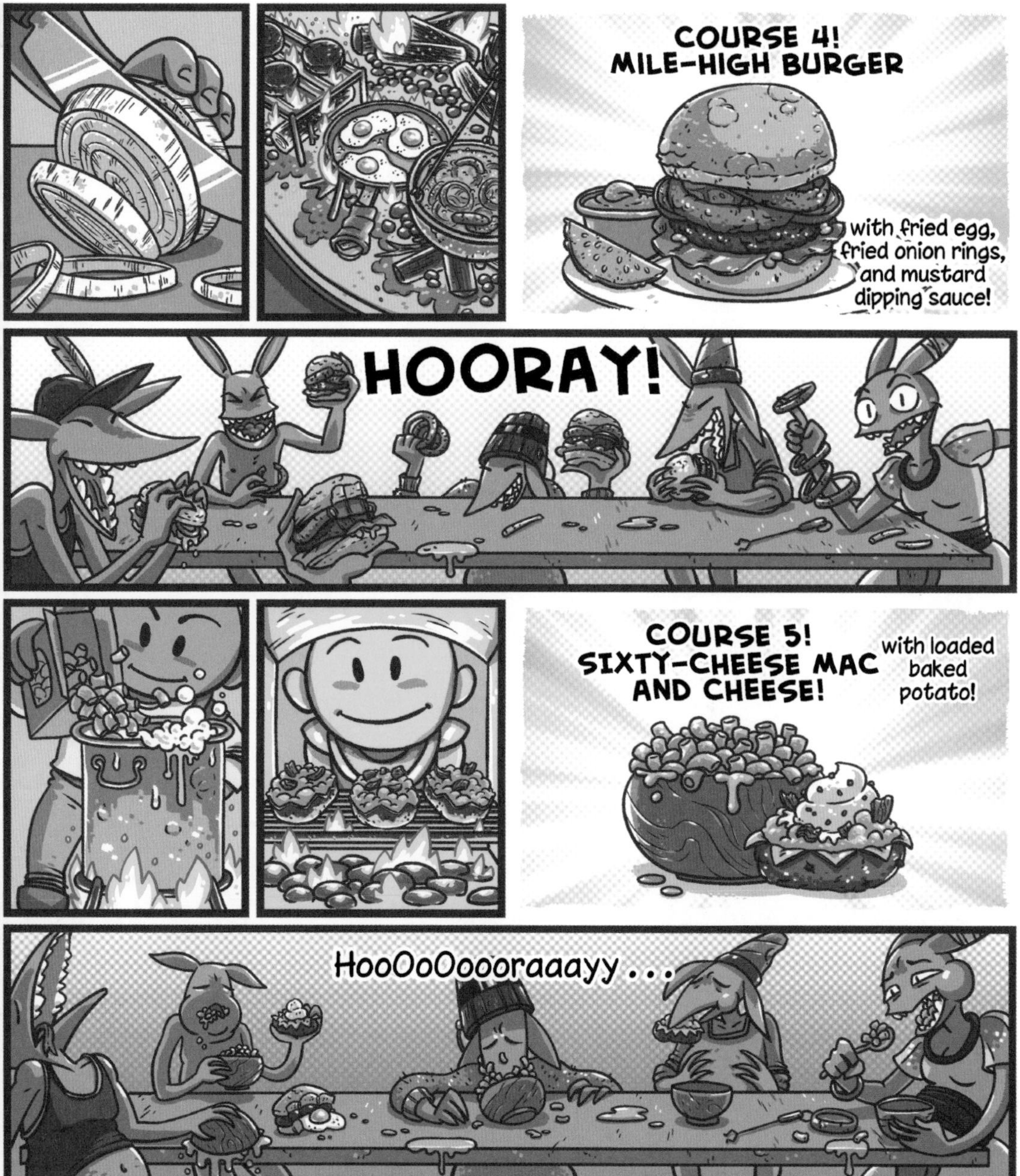
COURSE 4!
MILE-HIGH BURGER
with fried egg, fried onion rings, and mustard dipping sauce!
HOORAY!
COURSE 5!
SIXTY-CHEESE MAC AND CHEESE!
with loaded baked potato!
HooOoOoooraaayy . . .

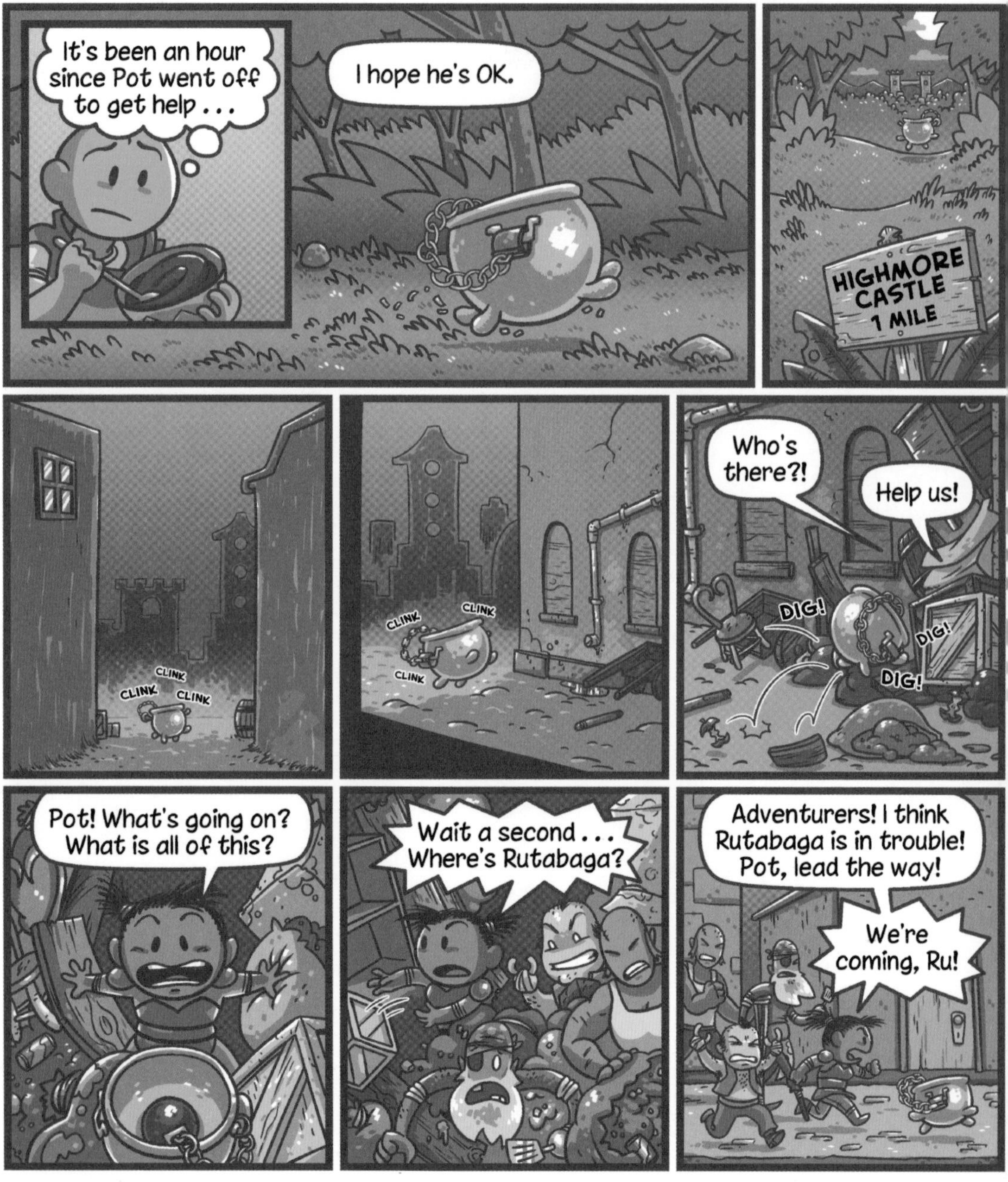
It's been an hour since Pot went off to get help . . .
I hope he's OK.
HIGHMORE CASTLE 1 MILE
CLINK
CLINK
CLINK
CLINK
CLINK
CLINK
Who's there?!
Help us!
DIG!
DIG!
DIG!
Pot! What's going on? What is all of this?
Wait a second . . . Where's Rutabaga?
Adventurers! I think Rutabaga is in trouble! Pot, lead the way!
We're coming, Ru!

End of Chapter Four

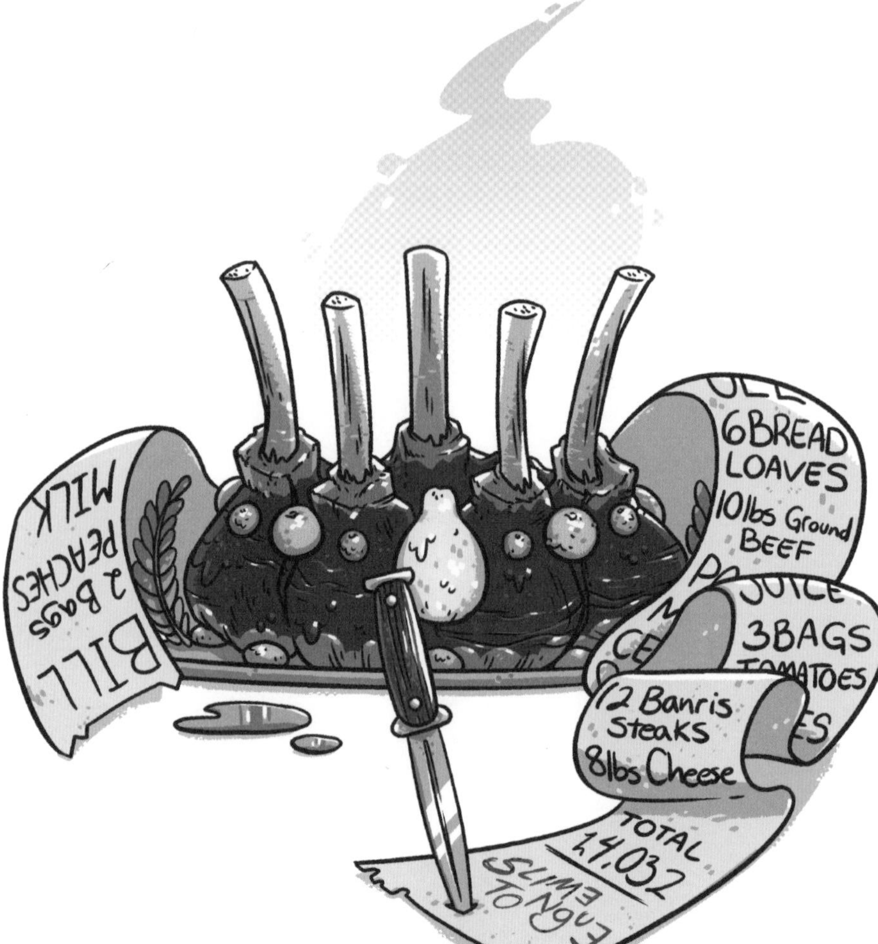

MILK
PEACHES
2 Bags
BILL
6 BREAD
LOAVES
10lbs Ground
BEEF
JUICE
3BAGS
TOMATOES
12 Banris
Steaks
8lbs Cheese
TOTAL
14,032

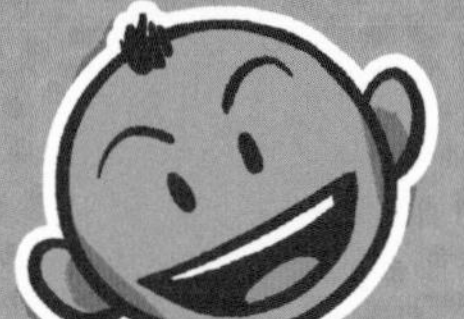

POPPING CHOCOLATE SPIDERS!

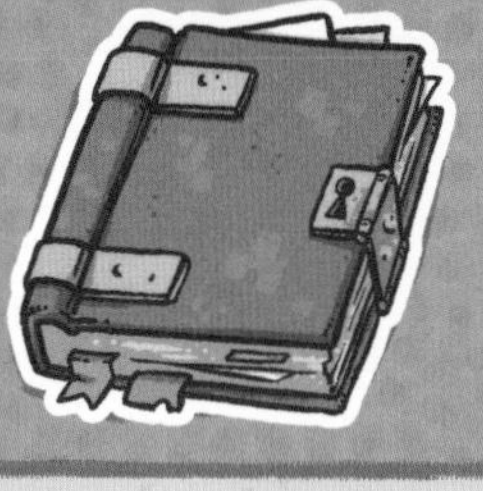

INGREDIENTS

- chocolate melts
- seedless grapes
- plastic sandwich bags
- chocolate sprinkles
- parchment or waxed paper

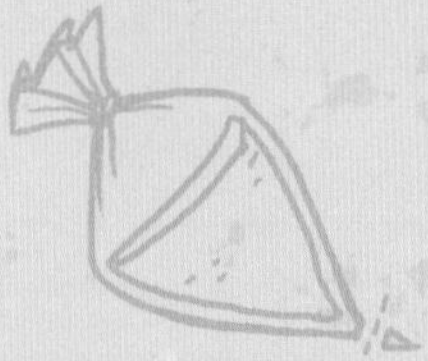

Wash and FULLY DRY the grapes! Even a tiny drop of water will ruin the chocolate! Let the grapes come to room temperature.

STOP! GET AN ADULT'S HELP WHEN HEATING ANYTHING IN THE MICROWAVE OR ON THE STOVE!

Melt chocolate according to package instructions.

Place a few heaping spoonfuls of chocolate into the corner of a plastic sandwich bag.

Snip off the tip of the plastic bag with a pair of scissors.

Place the parchment paper on a baking pan. With a steady hand, draw spider legs on the paper by squeezing the bag VERY GENTLY and piping the chocolate onto the paper. This will take some practice! Use the design on the right if you need help!

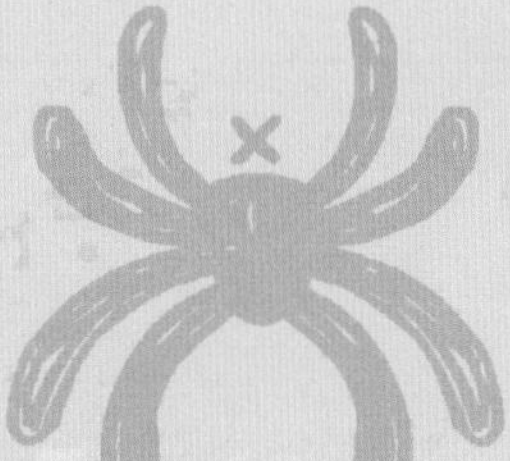
X
spider design!

After you've drawn a few spider legs, drop a grape in the leftover chocolate and coat it. Use a spoon to swoosh it around in the chocolate and place it on the back end of the spider legs, where the X is in the diagram. Repeat until all the spiders have butts.

Sprinkle chocolate sprinkles all over the spider butts while they're still wet!

Refrigerate for a few minutes and then carefully remove them from the parchment paper!

You have made

POPPING CHOCOLATE SPIDERS!

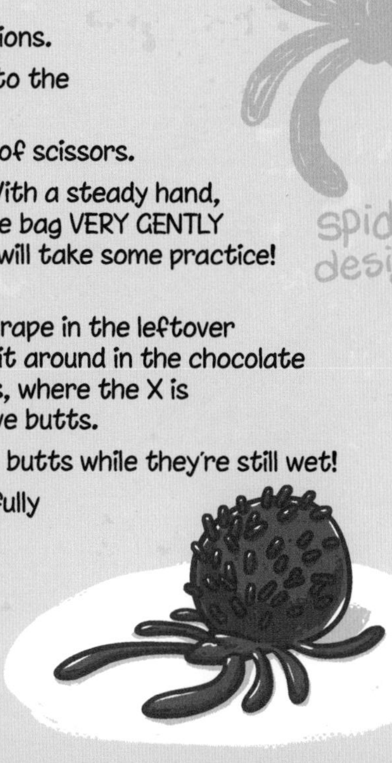

GUBBLIN SNOT!

INGREDIENTS

- 1 ripe kiwi
- 3/4 cup lemon-lime soda
- 3/4 cup pineapple juice
- 1/4 cup coconut milk

Chop the kiwi in half and squeeze the insides of one of the halves into a tall glass. Be careful not to let any of the kiwi skin slip into the drink!

Take a fork and smash the kiwi by pressing it into the sides of the glass. Really smoosh it up! Get it good and goopy!

Pour the pineapple juice and the lemon-lime soda into the glass.

Slowly pour the coconut milk over the mixture.

Take the fork and give it a few quick stirs so the soda fizzes up and makes the coconut milk a little frothy. Don't let it foam up too much and spill!

Finally, drink up!

You have made

GUBBLIN SNOT!

NO-BAKE "POISONED" COOKIES!

INGREDIENTS

- 1 3/4 cups granulated sugar
- 1/2 cup milk
- 8 tablespoons butter, cut into large pieces
- 3 tablespoons unsweetened cocoa powder
- 1 teaspoon vanilla extract
- 1/4 teaspoon salt
- 3 cups quick cooking oats
- green jelly beans
- parchment or waxed paper

Add sugar, milk, butter, and cocoa powder to a medium saucepan.

STOP! GET AN ADULT'S HELP WHEN HEATING ANYTHING IN THE MICROWAVE OR ON THE STOVE!

Over medium-high heat, bring to a boil for about three minutes.

Remove from heat and stir in vanilla, salt, and oats.

With a spoon, drop large scoops of the mixture onto parchment paper.

Press them flat with the spoon so they look like little pancakes.

Select a few cookies and place a green jelly bean in the center.

This cookie is now "POISONED"!

Fold each cookie in half, making sure the jelly beans are hidden!

Place the cookies on the counter or in the fridge until firm.

You have made

NO-BAKE "POISONED" COOKIES!

ACK!

If you eat a "poison" cookie, show everyone how good of an actor you are! Really ham it up!

ERIC COLOSSAL is an artist living and working in Upstate New York. His great loves are his cats, Juju and Bear; his lovely girlfriend, Jess; and eating. He is currently looking for a group of brave adventurers who will help him defeat whatever is making that horrible smell in the back of his fridge.